Amy Redek

Foxhole
Vixen of my Dreams
Erotic Bisexual Romance

Please feel free to send me an email. Just know that these emails are filtered by my publisher. Good news is always welcome.

Amy Redek - **amy_redek@awesomeauthors.org**

You might also want to check my blog for Updates and interesting info.
http://amy-redek.awesomeauthors.org/

About the Publisher
4Fun Publishing, a member of **BLVNP Incorporated,** 340 S. Lemon #6200, Walnut CA 91789, info@blvnp.com / legal@blvnp.com
NOTE: Due to the highly emotional reaction of some people to works of erotic fiction, any email sent to the above address that contains foul language or religious references is automatically deleted by our anti-spam software and will not be seen. All other communications are welcome.

DISCLAIMER
Please don't be stupid and kill yourself. This book is a work of FICTION. Do not try any new sexual practice that you find in this book. It is fiction and not to be confused with reality. Neither the author nor the publisher or its associates assume any responsibility for any loss, injury, death or legal consequences resulting from acting on the contents in this book. Every character in this book is over 18 years of age. The author's opinions are not to be construed as the opinions of the publisher. The material in this book is for entertainment purposes ONLY. Enjoy.

FOXHOLE

Vixen of my Dreams
Erotic Bisexual Romance

By: Amy Redek

©Amy Redek 2014
ISBN: 978-1-62761-861-8

IF I had asserted myself at the very beginning of my marriage, I would not be in the state of finding myself.

It would be better if I laid it all down along the line. You would see where I went wrong and used a phrase that fitted the bill, and that "Hindsight is the best viewing platform."

My name is Raymond Fox. I came from a middle class family based in Southampton. That's where my parents live and where I was brought up and educated until I went to a University to take up major in mathematics and banking systems. As a child, I showed a remarkable aptitude for numbers and it was suggested that my future should be in the Stock Market. But even though the money to be made on the floor was quite substantial, if one was lucky, it could also be a bubble that eventually would burst with those who chose this route if they didn't get out in time. I had my sights on more of a long term position in the banking world, not making as much money, but a steady progression to doing so from such a stable profession.

I earned my master's degree at twenty one and was lucky to obtain a position with Charter's Bank, a local branch in Southampton, at the lowest position and worked there for eight years, slowly moving up until I was offered a position of Assistant Manager at a branch in Oxford. It was at my last interview that I met the Chairman of Charter's Bank, Sir Eugene Charter, the fifth member of this family whose great, great grandfather had founded this banking empire in the city. I came to get very close to him later as you will see. He was the senior member of the board of five who were present at this interview, me being one of the last four being asked a series of questions about banking and my aims within the company. It lasted just over an hour and it was a really serious occasion with the astute questions being asked and it wasn't until a week later that I was summoned to the Head Office and told that I could now take over the management of their bank in Windsor.

My parents were delighted at this news even though I no longer lived in Southampton having moved out to lodgings in Oxford until now, and it was time to look for somewhere to live in the Windsor area. Not being a strong man in terms of my physique or in any other way except in the banking world, this position of manager really only required a quick mind in all the aspects of this profession, the handling of money and knowledge in the placing of it in the right places to make even more for the bank and its customers.

I did well there and got on with the staff under my control and it was a happy atmosphere and a pleasure to be working with such an amiable work force. I had been there for nearly a year when I received my invitation to attend an annual dinner of all the managers of the branches from all over the U.K. This was to be held at the Cumberland Hotel in Park Lane, London.

Suitably attired in my dinner suit, I attended and was just one of over a hundred other managers, some with their wives as well as the members of the company's board of directors. It was not only to hear speeches of how the bank was doing financially and a dinner but also there would be dancing, for which I silently thanked my mother in teaching me at an early age at how to conduct myself in the art of being able to dance well.

On entering the ballroom, I was greeted by Sir Eugene and after shaking his hand, was introduced to his wife, Lady Elizabeth whose hand I took and gallantly kissed the back of it as one did in the presence of royalty or persons of a higher standing. She smiled back at me and gave a short curtsey and introduced me to her daughter, Vivienne whose hand I took and kissed too, getting a deeper curtsey and an even bigger smile. Little did I know of her mind and even to this day, known as little now as I did then.

The dinner itself was excellent and I was very embarrassed at a part of the speech from Sir Eugene when he called out my name, asking me to stand as he presented me to all those gathered there saying that I was now the youngest and newest member of our bank. There was a lot of clapping of hands and with a very red face, gave a small bow in acknowledgement before sitting down to receive congratulations from those sitting at the same table as myself.

With the meal and speeches over, we were invited to move through to the ballroom for the dancing, where there were many small tables set around the floor with a large one at the far end which was for the directors and their wives to sit at during these dances. As people settled down at any other table, I was beckoned over by Sir Eugene.

'Well young man,' he began. 'As our newest and youngest manager, we are giving you the honour to open the dancing with Lady Elizabeth.' I felt my face redden at this and saw the smiles on the faces of the others seated at the table. There was nothing I could do but offer my arm to Lady Elizabeth and escort her out onto the floor and with a bow to her as she curtsied, the musicians started to play and we began the waltz to begin the dancing. After a turn around the floor, others started to join in and was soon filled with other men waltzing their partners.

Again, I silently thanked my mother at being able to dance without putting a foot wrong and at the end, escorted her back to the table and invited their daughter, Vivienne for the next dance. This was a quick step and I'm sure she deliberately moved her leg tight in between mine at every turn and sure she felt the reaction at me having this beautiful young woman in my arms. I even had her quite large breasts press up close to me which caused me some confusion at knowing she could feel the erection I had inside my trousers at this close bodily contact.

She sweetly smiled at me at the end of the dance, her eyes shining and it was rather erotic to see the way the tip of her tongue moved over her lips in a brief sweeping motion before I escorted her back to her table. I was glad to sit down and take a big gulp of my drink and hoped that I could sit out the next dance until I had deflated somewhat. It did and I danced with several other ladies at my table and in between, couldn't ignore the beckoning finger of Vivienne for me to go over and have another dance with her with the same result to my body. In fact, I had four dances with her all told and I knew that her method of dancing with me was deliberate, just to arouse me for her own amusement to see and feel my discomfort.

I was glad when the dancing came to an end and people started to leave and managed to lose myself with the others and get away. It was nearly an hour later that I was able to get undressed in my lodgings and get into bed and, with the thought of my dancing with Vivienne, got an erection and had to masturbate before I could get off to sleep.

IT WAS two months later that I received a letter in our bank's post that held an engraved invitation to attend a weekend gathering at CharterHouse, the home of the Charter family out in the Cotswolds. Vivienne told me later that it was her who had suggested the weekend party as she had told her parents that she had been rather taken with the shy youngest manager at the dance and would like to get to know him, me, a little better. She did too.

I duly turned up on the appointed day and was greeted by her and Sir Eugene and had a footman show me up to the room I would be occupying during the weekend. It was when having drinks before dinner that I was noted that there would be twelve sitting down and also found that I'm going to be sitting next to Vivienne.

The table talk was of a general matter, me hardly saying a word and I'm sure I would have stuttered if I spoke too long for I constantly had the thigh of Vivienne pressing against mine throughout the meal. I learned that the next afternoon would be a shooting party which I declined to attend not having ever handled a shotgun before and was sure that I would have made a fool of myself if I had tried. I was glad when dinner was over and the males of the party retired to the smoking room where some of them started on cigars along with their brandy. I didn't smoke and soon made my apologies saying that I was tired and had another footman escort me up to my bedroom.

Alone at last, I got undressed and had a shower before cleaning my teeth and naked, got into the large bed that dominated the room and it wasn't long before I was asleep. But not for long for I was woken up by hearing the door to my room being closed and I sat up.

'Who's there?' I queried into the darkness.

'Me. Vivienne,' came the reply and heard the whisper of clothing as she came to the bed and felt the cover being pulled back and had her naked body slide in and move up close to me. A heavy breast was pressed against my arm as a hand came onto my chest to give it a sweeping motion. 'I couldn't wait to come and find out if you are as big as I felt when we danced,' she said as the hand moved from chest and down over my stomach to find that I had risen up at feeling the contact of her breast against my arm. 'Oooh, you are,' she breathed out as her hand curled round my erection that had sprung up at our body contact and I started to sweat. This was because I'd only ever had one woman before and that was at a drunken party at the University and couldn't really remember at how I managed to fuck her, nor know her name. I'm glad that Vivienne took over.

'Raymond? Will you use this on me? Well in me really. It's nice and big and I want to feel it inside me.' So, being the gentleman I was, turned and got my body across hers as she opened her legs for me to get in between. Her breasts I squashed a bit with my chest before I lifted myself up onto my elbows and moved up and felt the head of my cock unerringly find its way into the slippery warmth of her body, moving in until our pubes met and heard her give out a big sigh and felt her internal muscles start to squeeze me, making my cock twitch before I started to move in my first fuck of her.

'Oh Raymond, I love this,' she panted as I moved myself inside her, her arms up and her hands gripping my shoulders as she began to get into the same rhythm as myself, but such was my desire to please her, I started to come too soon and was really ramming myself into her as I started to give her my semen. 'Yes, yes, yes,' she moaned at every spurt that I sent into her until I came to a stop, breathing rather heavily.

'You didn't cum,' I panted, feeling her hard nipples brushing my chest with every intake of breath.

'No. You came too soon. Maybe next time with you now having come once, it will probably be slower,' and gave out a little cry as I eased myself up, feeling her trying to hold my erection from slipping out of her. As I rolled onto my back as she too rolled, but onto her side and kissed me.

'Will you go down on me now?' she asked.

'Go down? Down where?' I was that green in those days as regards to having sex with a woman.

'Between my legs and suck me,' she said, and I thought I caught a touch of petulance in her voice.

'Oh,' I said, not really knowing what was expected of me in regards of this, but I moved and slid down the bed and in between her legs, moving by touch really for I couldn't see in the dark. I felt her pubic hairs with my chin and knew I was close and moved down a little more, smelling her fragrance and found the lips of her vagina with my tongue. Not really knowing what to do, I pushed my tongue between the soft lips and found her all wet inside as I ran my tongue around the insides and felt a small nodule and felt her give out a shiver as my tongue touched it. This I guessed was what she wanted and so kept flicking my tongue against it as well as running the tip over it as she moaned and felt her legs trying to come together at my doing this.

How long does she want me to do this I thought? Moving my tongue further round and guessed that I had found the entrance to her vagina where I could feel the most wetness. I managed to get some of my tongue inside this as she began to squirm and buck and had her thighs tightening themselves against my head and she then gave out a big shudder and I felt some hot fluid come down onto my tongue and some into my mouth.

So this was her orgasm, ran through my mind and found that it wasn't that bad, though it didn't say much for my prick if it was my tongue that gave her this orgasm.

It took some effort to prise her thighs away from my head for I was desperate to get some air into my lungs and took deep breaths when my face came free.

'Oh Raymond,' she moaned, tugging at my ears, making me then move back up her body to relieve the strain she was putting on them until I was back up on top of her, to have her pull my head down and kiss me quite passionately. 'That was just lovely Raymond,' she breathed into my ear. 'I really needed that,' glad that she'd broken off the kissing to speak for I needed air again.

I rolled myself off of her and did not just lie there, but kept a hand on one breast, moulding it and running the palm over the nipple that had now gone a little soft. Her hand also moved, but down the bed and took hold of my now limp dick and kept moving it about for a while until it started to get hard again.

I lasted longer this time as I mounted and fucked her for the second time, keeping up a slow rhythm until she began bucking beneath me and had her fingers digging deep into my shoulders as she began to have her second orgasm. I had been holding myself back a little this time and it was a relief to let go as she thrashed about as she came.

'That was much better this time,' she breathed out when I rolled off of her and had her stroking my still hard erection. 'We should do this again soon but I must go back to my room now,' and with her giving me a quick kiss, got out of bed and I could hear the rustle of what I thought must be her dressing gown being put on before she left me to go to sleep and dream of the woman I'd just had.

IN THE morning, after a shower and shaving among other things in the bathroom, got dressed and made my way down to the dining room where I found all the males getting their breakfast and being entertained by Vivienne.

'Good morning everybody,' I said when I entered the room and they chorused in reply with Vivienne jumping up from her chair.

'Good morning Raymond. My, I do seem rather perky this morning. Did you have a good night?' she asked with a smile, her eyes alight and saw her tongue whisper itself over her lips.

'Yes thank you. Best night I've had in ages,' I said and accepted her offer to get me my breakfast which she did, putting the full plate down next to where she had been sitting.

'Are you going shooting with the others?' she asked, sitting down next to me.

'No,' I mumbled through a mouthful of food. 'I'm not sure what to do.'

'Case settled,' she said. 'You can keep me company and see the house and grounds properly.' I had no answer to this and so, after breakfast, she gave me a tour of the house.

Now I hadn't really taken in the size of the place when I had first arrived and now found how magnificent it was and perfectly coordinated in the choice of furniture and the like, in all the rooms, and said as much, which appeared to please her as she smiled back.

We shared a light lunch out on one of the patios and I was given a tour of the gardens, finishing up at a small gazebo next to a miniature lake that, as she told me, had been filled with fish for her father and friends to fish out of the shooting season. We could hear the sounds of gunfire off in the distance of the shooting party as she took me inside where, among other things, was a chaise longue to which she pulled me.

Well it wasn't long before she had my hand inside her blouse to massage a breast, her not wearing a bra, and not long before I was on top of her and giving her another orgasm as we fucked there in the gazebo. Needless to say, she was back in my room for another session of us coupling that night and it quite exhausted me, fucking her twice as well as going down on her.

In some ways, it was a relief when the weekend finished and I gave my thanks to Sir Eugene and Lady Elizabeth as well as Vivienne for a lovely weekend as I said my goodbyes, but I then felt rather lonely when I was back in my lodgings in Windsor.

After that, I seemed to get an invite every other weekend to either go racing, of which Sir Eugene owned two racehorses, or a football match, him also being the owner of a football club. At each and every event I went to, I had Vivienne in attendance and I must say, she looked really gorgeous dressing up for a race meeting where one of her father's horses was running. Being a bank manager, I didn't believe in gambling and only used money on certain things, definitely not to be used on a race course. She seemed quite miffed when I said that I never backed horses, but eventually gave in and placed a bet on her father's horse, though she didn't know that I backed it each way and so when it came in second, I at least got back more than my stake money with the odds being twelve to one.

We didn't have sex during these outings but had her in my room sometime during the night and came to love having her in bed next to me, only having to roll over to fuck her instead of masturbating.

I was collared by Sir Eugene one evening after dinner, having our brandy. 'Well my boy, our Vivienne has taken quite a shine to you,' he said. 'She seems to want you up here as often as she can. What do you think or read into that?'

'Well sir. She's a very lovely forward girl and it's hard to resist any suggestions she makes,' thinking of my time in bed with her. 'I enjoy her company as much as I like coming here to see you and your wife.'

'Well said my boy, and thank you for the comments,' and I'm sure that he had a twinkle in his eyes at this and wondered if he knew or was guessing that I had slept, after a fashion, with her. But it later led him to ask me if I had any intentions towards her? His thought I could see was if I had marriage in mind and had my mouth speaking before my brain was in gear. For I then asked if he would agree to my courting of Vivienne with this intention and got a slap on the back and had his consent and that of his wife, he added.

So now having said it, I had to go along with it and eventually proposed to Vivienne and had her accept.

WHAT A lavish affair the wedding was. There must have been a hundred guests attending, most being from her side as I only had my parents and members of my staff from the bank on that Saturday morning. It was held in the church local to CharterHouse and the reception in the grounds of their mansion with two marquees and an orchestra. Plenty of food and drink for all the guests and mother and father lapped it up, me marrying into this obviously wealthy family. My assistant in the bank was my best man and did rather well in his speech at the reception, no doubt currying favour for me to put his name forward as a future manager of one of the branches, which I did eventually. We had many wedding gifts that were put out on display except for two, which were from my now father and mother-in-law, because one was a house in Windsor and a Bentley that would be ready when we returned from our honeymoon.

It had all been laid on by her father and after the reception, we changed into travelling clothes and were driven to Heathrow Airport and boarded a Lyons Airway plane that only carried twenty passengers and of all things, had a bedroom aboard, well two actually. It was only after takeoff that we were allowed into this small room that was filled with this flying mattress where we quickly got our clothes off and joined the mile high club.

It was lovely to be inside my new wife, fucking her as I looked out through the small window and could see the white clouds far below us and later, she was straddling me to get the same view as she fucked herself in this position on top of me.

We even got to sleep on this flying mattress and were quite perky when we landed at Nassau, only to get on another plane, one that can land on water, a seaplane. This was the ferry as it were, to Lyon Island, which boasted of having a beach where clothes were optional. In other words, a nudist beach. Vivienne was all for this and after having our gear placed in our room, went and visited this beach.

It was grand to lay there naked in the sun and watch the beautiful tits passing by though Vivienne remarked more on the men, comparing the size of their tackle as well as trying to guesstimate the weight of their balls. An hour was enough for our first day as we were already going rather red and so spent the rest of the day, it being five hours difference to England's time, in our room. The meals were superb and the staff most cordial and helpful, but we spent most of our time down on this special beach.

After a week, were both a nice golden brown and Vivienne cried off for the odd hour or two while I stayed there getting even browner while she went off to our room. I only found out a year or so later that during that second week, she had been having it off with two of the other guests as well as having one of the black members of staff fucking her while I was still sunning myself on the beach. I didn't know then that I had married a nymphomaniac and wanted sex as many times as she could get and didn't care the age, colour or creed of the man fucking her.

Well anyway, the honeymoon came to an end and we flew back to an indifferent climate in England and found that our new house had been fully furnished to suit her tastes. Unlike the mansion that she had previously lived in, we didn't have any servants, and I, having lived in lodgings, had learned to cook and so I did most of the cooking of our meals while she did the most minimal of housekeeping. This she did while I was back at work in the bank.

As promised by my now father-in-law Sir Eugene, a Bentley was there in the garage and this then replaced my old Ford that I had previously used. I felt quite proud of driving this new car to the bank, having my own private parking slot at the rear.

When the weekend came round, I usually stayed in bed a little longer and she gave me a surprise this first Saturday morning by getting up before me and said that she would see to bringing me breakfast in bed. Now that was the first surprise at offering to do this and I stayed there in anticipation and then got a second surprise when she brought in the tray for she had dressed herself up as a maid. I couldn't get over this and we had fun, after eating our breakfast there, of playing about on the bed in my seducing of this maid and fucking her there whilst still wearing her underwear.

What I didn't know that this was a prelude of getting me to dress up as the maid and serve her breakfast in bed which is what she wanted on the Sunday. I argued about this after our frolics on the bed but in the end, gave way and agreed to dress up as she wanted.

So later that afternoon, with both of us naked, she helped me get dressed in these female garments. Mind you, I found it quite erotic as I rolled the black stockings up my legs to fix them to the suspender belt she had helped fix around my waist. So erotic, that I got an erection at the feel of these stockings moving up my legs and had it sticking out in front of me as she helped me with the bra, padding the cups out with some handkerchiefs.

The dress was rather short for me, being somewhat taller than her, so you could get brief glimpses of the stocking tops as I moved. She even found a wig for me to wear so that the little cap could be fixed to the top and with the final pinny around my waist, I really looked like a female as I saw myself in the wardrobe mirror. This made my cock stick out even more and this could clearly be noted with the front of the dress pushed out in front of me.

So this was the way I was dressed the following morning as I made her breakfast and delivered it to our room and then had the fun of having her seduce me into having sex with me still wearing the underthings, the dress being the only item of clothing taken off.

I was in the middle of fucking her when she gave me a new name. 'With my surname now being Fox, this is what I am going to call you when you are dressed like a maid. Renard instead of Raymond, Renard being the French for fox,' she said.

I gave a few grunts before replying. 'With you now being a fox too, and being a female, you should be called Vixen instead of Vivienne.'

'The male fox is known as a dog,' she replied.

'Oh. Well let's leave it as Vivienne then,' I said, pushing myself harder into her as I came, feeling her squeeze my cock as I did so.

She gave out a big sigh as I pulled out and rolled over onto my back, and looking down my body, it seemed strange to see my cock, still hard, lying up on my stomach and almost touching the suspender belt. This looks rather silly, I thought to myself at seeing my stocking covered legs and the bra across my chest, but that is what she wanted, so be it.

I got up from the bed and picked up her breakfast things and put them on the tray, and as I moved past the end of the bed she called out. 'Renard,' and I turned around and saw the light flash on the camera she now had in her hand. Where she had got it from, I don't know, but she now had a picture of me inside the bedroom wearing this female attire and showing what I had between my legs.

'Vivienne no!' I cried, nearly losing the tray in my hand.

'Too late,' she laughed as she aimed it at me again and took another picture. I could only give her a grimace and turned to leave the bedroom, but I wasn't quick enough for her to take yet another one, showing my naked backside before I could get out of the door.

I must say that later when I saw these pictures on the computer, I could see that they weren't bad in an erotic way and so later, agreed to have some more pictures taken with me wearing the maid's dress too. Mind you, these pictures came back to bite me later.

So this became our practice every weekend that she would be the maid on the Saturday morning and I would get the thrill of donning this female garb on the Sunday and at her coaxing, stayed dressed like this for the rest of the day. She even got me a pinny to wear because when I prepared and cooked dinner, she insisted that I took the dress off so as not to get it splashed with oil or whatever, when cooking. So I would wear the underwear and have this pinny on so that I wouldn't drop anything hot down my front. She took another picture of me like this and it looked rather funny seeing the long white tapes of the pinny hanging down between the cheeks of my bare bum. She even took a couple of me full frontal when I had an erection and these looked most incongruous being dressed as a female and yet have an erect cock sticking out in front of me.

It was a couple of months later when I was in the bank that I damaged my left hand. The vault had been opened but I saw it begin to close and guessed that it hadn't been fixed to the fitting that held it open. I pushed the door back and was using my left hand to lift the catch that fitted over the handle to hold it in place, but I pushed a bit too hard and went and got my hand caught between this handle and the catch. Now the door is not a light one and is of a considerable weight and couldn't help giving out a cry as my hand got trapped in the catch.

It took two assistants to help me get my hand out, one easing the door slightly while the other lifted the latch to get my hand out. Christ did it hurt! I had tears in my eyes at the pain and was glad to have a chair placed behind me to sit down on or I think I would have keeled over. I sat there holding my left hand with my right, fighting to hold the tears back as I looked at the blood on my hand and the fast swelling that was appearing through it.

'Shall I call an ambulance?' one of the girls asked.

'No,' I said through gritted teeth. 'Just a taxi to take me to the hospital.'

This was done and I gave instructions to my assistant manager to see to the locking up the bank as I didn't think I would get back from the hospital till after closing. Also be prepared to open the next day in case I didn't turn up. This he agreed to do and wished me well as I left when the taxi arrived.

I was in the hospital three hours where they first gave me some pain killers and then cleaned the hand for x-rays and found that I hadn't broken anything apart from the skin and it would show up heavily bruised later. They put some creams on it before putting bandages and told me to go home and rest it.

I got a taxi just outside of the hospital and decided not to go to the bank but straight home even though there was still another couple of hours before closing time. This dropped me off outside my house and I went indoors.

'Is that you Raymond?' Vivienne called down from upstairs.

'Yes dear,' I replied.

'You're early. Well as you are, be Renard and bring up a pot of coffee and two cups please,' she said before I heard the door of the bedroom then close.

Oh shit, I said to myself, but shrugged my shoulders and went up to the spare room and got out the maid's underwear and dress as well as the wig and cap before I took my clothes off to put these on. It took some time with having my damaged hand virtually useless in doing this, but I managed, knowing that I would get all kinds of sympathy when she saw it.

So dressed up as the maid, I went back downstairs and made the coffee and when it was ready, put it on a tray with two cups, milk and sugar and took it upstairs. It was a bit of a job balancing the tray to get the door open, but I did and went inside and nearly dropped the tray.

For there in bed with Vivienne was another man! My eyes must have almost popped out of their sockets at seeing her sitting up, bare breasted and this other man lying next to her showing his bare chest.

'Wha....what....what the fuck is he doing there?' I stuttered, now feeling very foolish to be standing there dressed as a maid and trying not to lose the tray I was holding. 'And why is he in bed with you?' A foolish question to ask when you come to think of it.

'Well at the moment, he's resting,' she said without the slightest qualm in speaking the way she was. 'He's just been fucking me, and it was great! Look!' and she flipped down the sheet that was covering this man's lower body and saw that he had an erection that was quite big, lying up on his stomach. 'Big isn't he?' I'm sure my face had gone quite red at seeing her, and him, lying in bed there and now also seeing the big cock that he had just fucked her with out in full view.

'But....but....You're .....,' was all I managed to get out as she interrupted me before I could utter the words, "my wife."

'Yes, and you are my maid and this is Richard, my lover,' she said in such a calm voice that you would have thought that she was reading a script or something to appear so blasé about it. What made it look worse was that she then began stroking this man's cock. 'I'm sorry Richard, but we'll have to call it a day now that he's come home earlier than expected.' And she astounded me again by leaning over and giving him a kiss. I could have thrown the tray at him as he kissed her back and moved, and got out of bed. The cheek of the bastard was that he smiled at me as he stood up, bollock naked as he did so, and I'm glad that I still held the tray and not thrown it at him and hit him with my right hand. Because I would have lost that fight hands down for he stood at least a few inches up over six foot and built like a brick shithouse.

I could only stand there and watch as he put his clothes on before bending back over the bed and giving Vivienne another kiss. 'Till tomorrow then,' he said in a strong voice and turned to me as he left.

'Nice to have met you Renard,' he smirked as he went out and heard him go downstairs and out of the front door.

I was lost for words, still standing there like some dumb statue looking back at Vivienne, my wife, who had been fucking another man while I was at work.

'How….how could you?' I finally managed to croak out.

'You were at work and I was bored,' she said, patting that part of the bed where this man had laid. 'Sit down and let us have some coffee.' I couldn't help myself but move over and sit down, placing the tray on her lap and it was only then that she noticed my bandaged hand.

'Oh, what have you done?' she cried, nearly upsetting the tray, her tits wobbling very nicely. The tits that that man had probably sucked on which made my anger rise up again.

'What do you care!' I cried. 'I get hurt at work and you are home having it off with a strange man.'

'He's not a strange man as you say. He plays for daddy's football team. He's the right back,' she answered me.

'He should be, right back where he came from. How could you?'

'Well you were at work and I needed a man, so I gave him a ring.'

'You gave him a ring and he came running' I sneered.

'Yes. They all do when I want them to,' she spat back at me.

'All!? How many have you had?'

'I've lost count,' she smiled sweetly at me.

'Lost count!?' I almost screamed at her.

'When the daughter of their boss tells them she wants to be fucked, they don't argue and come, in more ways than one,' she sniggered.

'You…you….'

'Slut?' she interrupted me. 'Is that the word you're looking for? Don't say whore because I'll throw this coffee over you. I don't take money from them, just their sperm. And nice sperm it is, you should try some yourself.'

'You mean you even suck on their cocks?' I asked in an incredulous way.

'Oh yes, especially when they've just pulled out of me. Then I get to taste both the man and myself at the same time.'

'You've never sucked on mine,' I stated.

'You've never asked. But if you were to go down on me now, I'll then suck on you.'

'But you've just had another man's prick up there,' I cried.

'So what? You'll not know the difference. You might even like it so it's either suck on me or not for I won't go down on you if you don't.'

Wild thoughts had been running through my brain while she was saying these words and the thing was, my own cock had been rising up at hearing this and was now like a rigid flagpole, pushing out the front of this maid's dress I was wearing. This she had noticed and put her hand out and grasped it through the material.

'I can see and feel that the thought of me sucking on you has turned you on. Well, do you go down on me or what?'

I didn't want to know of to what, for I really did want to see and feel those lips of hers around the head of my cock as she sucked on me. Would she swallow my sperm or spit it out? You'll never know if you don't, said the voice in my head, so suck her and see.

'The…the tray's in the way,' I stammered after listening to that little voice.

'The coffee's probably cold by now anyway,' she said, picking it up and leaning over her side of the bed, placed the tray on the floor. 'Take the dress off first,' she said as she pushed down the sheet to bare her legs and let me see where I was going to go.

I got up off the bed and pulled the dress up over my head, taking the wig off at the same time before getting back onto the bed and moving in between her open legs. It was much better doing this in the dark and not actually seeing the inside of a females genitalia, but, as I wanted her to suck on me, closed my eyes as I parted the lips of her labia and began sticking my tongue inside.

It was wet and I'm sure that some of this wetness was semen from that bloody man that had fucked her earlier, but it didn't offend my taste buds, so kept on moving my tongue about, especially over the bud of her clitoris. This was obviously the right thing to do for she gave out a little start at the first touch and began to groan and twitch the more I did so.

I managed to get my shoulders between her thighs this time so when she tried to clamp my head, she couldn't, so I was able to lift it slightly to get some air into my lungs as I plated her. More pressure came to my shoulders as she started to move her body, pushing herself to me as my tongue kept moving in and out of her vagina, rasping the clit in the process. Boy, did she buck about or not as she approached her orgasm? But I managed to stay there as she gave out one big shudder and I felt some of her juices come down to my mouth. No doubt bringing some more of that man's semen along with it.

By now I had a raging hard on and with her coming to a stop in her moving about, got myself out from between her thighs and worked my way up her body, wiping my mouth across her stomach in the process.

'That was just great Renard,' she said with a big smile on her face as she pulled me right up on top of her, squashing those lovely tits against my chest as she kissed me.

'Now your turn to suck on me,' I said as we broke off the kiss, my piece throbbing away like mad.

'Later dear,' she said.

'What!' I reared up. 'You said that if I went down on you that you would then suck on me.'

'Well I will if you also agree that Richard can come tomorrow.' I was flabbergasted at this.

'He came today, and I'm sure that I got a taste of him while down on you,' I said rather petulantly. 'With my hand as it is, I was going to stay at home tomorrow.'

'You can stay at home if you want to, and you can also watch him fucking me if you would like to,' she said in a sly voice. 'Say yes and I'll even suck your balls.'

I was in a cleft stick for I really did need her to suck on my throbbing cock and it was even harder and paining me now at what she had suggested about me watching this other man fuck her. There must have been some kind of depravity in me that urged me to say yes and yet….. Oh Christ!

'Ye…yes,' I stuttered.

'You're a good man,' she said, her eyes shining as she pushed me over onto my back and quickly moved herself over and lay on my thigh and took hold of my erection in a firm grasp looking up at me as she licked her lips. I lay there, tense, waiting for her mouth to open and take in the head of my cock, but she didn't move.

'You'll also be dressed as you are now in the bedroom?' she asked.

'That's blackmail!' I cried.

'I know, and if I let him fuck me doggie fashion, I can then suck on you at the same time,' she leered. That was it.

'Yes, yes, yes. Now suck on me,' I cried, and saw that lovely mouth open and had the thrill of having those lips I kiss close around beneath the head of my erection as it was engulfed in the heat of her mouth. I couldn't help but give out a gasp at this first time of having her where she was and trembled throughout my body as her tongue moved over the raw flesh as she worked the foreskin right down to be able to tongue the G string. It was some kind of heaven to feel her doing this to me, and more so as her hand began to move up and down exciting me even more, the throbbing of my left hand just a minor irritation at this time.

It wasn't long before I felt my seed start to move and began to buck my hips up as she sucked and as I erupted in her mouth, it also felt as if she was pulling it up by the suction. Her hand kept moving and squeezing as she helped it on its way and didn't stop until she felt my body relax back on the bed. I could see her head moving and as she turned it sideways to look up at me, I could see the bulge in her cheek of my cock head and also her Adam's apple move as she swallowed what she held in her mouth.

She hadn't finished either, for after lifting her head up off of me, letting what felt like cold air waft around and over the exposed flesh of my cock's head, she nibbled her way down the underside of my still erect cock. She stopped nibbling when she got down to my balls and I had the thrill of feeling her take the whole sac into her mouth and have the plum like testicles be moved about with her tongue.

What heaven this was I thought as many emotions ran through my body, my mind forgetting what was to happen the next day because of these ministrations I was getting from her, they only came to mind later. She finally released me and came sliding up my body, the nipples of her tits almost cutting two lines up my chest they were that hard and pointed.

'There, now wasn't that good or not?' she asked before she kissed me. I could only say yes to this as she then rolled off of me and then noticing the bandage on my left hand again. 'Oh you poor thing,' she cried, holding it and stroking my wrist, asked me to tell her how it happened.

She was then, and for the rest of the afternoon and evening, most solicitous about it, cooking the dinner herself and even opening a wine bottle as I was unable to perform this task. I had taken my pain killers earlier and it wasn't so bad now even though it was still throbbing.

Because I had stayed in Reynard, the maid's underwear but with the small pinny at the front, she stayed naked and also donned another pinny to wear when preparing the evening meal. We also had a good fucking session when we finally went to bed, though I didn't go down on her or give her another orgasm but come myself I did.

IT WAS my throbbing hand that woke me up in the morning and was surprised to find that I had gotten into bed and had sex with Vivienne before falling asleep, still wearing the female underwear. She woke up with my moving about and even got up first and went downstairs to make the coffee and bring it back up.

'We might as well keep these things here,' she said as she helped me get the underwear off so that I could have a shower, 'and you can put them back on afterwards as you'll have to wear them this afternoon. With the dress and wig too,' she added.

My heart sank at her recalling for me what I had said that I would do, and I cringed inside at the very thought of watching another man fuck her. The only credit side of this was that she would suck on me at the same time but still couldn't believe that I had agreed to this, and so it was with some trepidation that I waited for the afternoon to come round. Vivienne made sure that I was wearing the maid's underwear. Helping me with this and seeing that the dress was on properly and the wig and cap in place. For I was expected to act the part of the maid in letting him into the house and seeing to the drinks that they both would have. Then I would have to stay in the bedroom to watch the two start this farce.

I felt absolutely stupid and silly and somewhat degraded at having to answer the door bell when it rang. Vivienne was already upstairs in the bedroom and I went and answered the door to find this man Richard standing outside.

'Hello Renard,' he said with a smile on his face as he entered and all I could do was nod my head in acknowledgement, seething inside. 'Where's Vivienne?'

'Upstairs in the bedroom, waiting for you,' I said. I had really meant to say this with a surly voice but it didn't come out that way and felt ashamed at not being able to with this hulk of man standing next to me. 'This way,' I said, stupidly saying this I know as I led the way upstairs for he knew damn well where the bedroom was, but it was done and I got to the bedroom door and knocked before opening it. 'Your, er, guest has arrived,' I managed to get out and stood aside as he entered with me then moving in too and closing the door behind me.

'Vivienne! You look gorgeous in that,' he said and I now saw that she was wearing a see through peignoir that I hadn't seen before.

'You'd look gorgeous too if you were out of those clothes,' she said, moving over to him and taking him into her arms and kissed him. If looks could kill, he would have been dead there on his feet with daggers in his back as he held her in his arms, kissing her back with quite some passion. As I was off to one side, I saw one of his hands move up and squeeze one of her tits before she pushed him away.

'Get those clothes off first,' she said to him as she moved towards the bed.

'What about Renard there?' he asked, looking at me still standing near the door.

'Renard's being given the privilege of watching us and taking a small part. Renard!' she said quite sharply. 'Come over here near the head and take that dress off.' Being the slave and fool that I was, went over near the bed's headboard and eased the dress off my shoulders and let it slip slowly to the floor. I'm sure that my face was red as I did this, for it certainly felt that it was. Of course, as soon as the dress fell below my waist, revealed to Richard that I was a male dressed up in this female attire.

He had started to laugh but on seeing my face, turned it into a cough.

'Well that something you don't see every day. I must say Renard that you fooled me. He's going to watch us?' he asked, turning to Vivienne who was taking off her peignoir.

'Yes, and I've promised to suck on him while you fuck me. It'll have to be in the doggie fashion Richard. Now get those clothes off and come to bed,' she said as she pulled the covers down and got on herself. She looked the most perfect woman as she settled herself down and watched, as I did, Richard take off his clothes. These he threw onto a chair as he stripped off and he was as big in stature as he was the day before and had his cock in an upright position that was revealed when his pants came off.

I was mesmerized to see it sway before him as he moved to the bed and then bounce up and down as he got on and lay alongside Vivienne. He's lying on your side of the bed my little voice in my head said, and he's doing the same as what you do, as I watched his hand come onto a tit and start to massage it. I could feel the nipple rise that he felt but saw the other one rise up to the other hand's manipulation of the one he was fondling.

But my eyes moved off that tit and were drawn to look at his erection that was half on her bare leg, the head partly exposed from the stretched foreskin and looking quite red. I can't explain it, but seeing it lying there and knowing that it would soon be inside my wife, made my own cock start to rise up.

For a minute or two his hand had moved down between her open legs and guessed that he had his fingers up inside her as she kept moving her body about before she pushed his hand away.

'Now Richard. Move over and let me get on my knees.' This he did and I was watching his cock move about more than at Vivienne as she turned on the bed on her hands and knees, one hand waving me towards the lower half of the bed. I moved down till I was opposite her backside, watching Richard move across one of her legs as he got between them. His cock kept moving with slight jerks and guessed that it was really throbbing now and watched as he put the head to her wet pussy and saw it slowly start to disappear inside her. I wanted to scream out that it was my cunt that he was sticking his dick into, but kept silent as it went fully in as far as it could go, his thighs up tight to the cheeks of her bum.

Out of the corner of my eye, I saw her hand wave again, but moving up towards the top and so I moved myself and saw that I was fully rigid and only then felt the throbbing that it was giving out to the rest of my body. As I moved in closer to the bed, I saw Richard, kneeling upright, start to move and knew that his cock was now sliding in and out of her and looked at her and saw that she was opening her mouth and so moved it the last bit and had the hot insides cover the head of my raging erection.

It was a bit awkward in this position with her head bent towards me as she tried to suck, her head and body moving backwards and forwards to Richard's thrusting inside her from the rear. My cock was being pulled from side to side with this motion and nearly coming out at some points. But it was still erotic at seeing her being fucked by another man as my own cock was being seen to by her mouth and tongue. This brought me quite quickly up to the point of no return and had to try and hold her head steady as I started cumming, sending out my semen in short sharp bursts. I nearly laughed when her eyes crossed at the first surge into her mouth but controlled myself as I now held her firmly to give her all that I had before letting go. Her face was quite red and it seemed difficult for her to swallow my cumming but managed it

With me being finished with, I turned my attention to Richard, who, with his head thrown back, his eyes closed, kept up his movements and I moved further down and saw the cheeks of his bum rather tight, slightly wobbling as his hips moved backwards and forwards and his hands gripping her hips in a tight grasp, then with a sudden stiffening of his spine, his buttocks seemed to clench themselves even tighter as his hips gave short sharp rams into Vivienne as he must have then started to cum and with each forward bump of his hips, sent another surge of semen up into her vagina. Hope she's on the pill was the stupid thought that crossed my mind as I watched him come to a stop and lean over her rear end and now heard him panting with Vivienne crooning and then giving out a little cry as I saw his wet and glistening cock being pulled out of her.

His body posture had slumped a little when he was out and it looked as if he keeled over as he moved to one side and twisting his body to land on his back, his still erect and wet cock making a slapping noise as it finished up on his stomach. Vivienne was quick in moving too as she rose up and moved downwards slightly and lifted up his wet cock and took the head of it into her mouth. She was obviously getting the sperm left over inside his cock as well as taking some of her own internal fluids in as she sucked on him.

I was like a spare prick at a wedding at seeing this, my own cock throbbing again as I stood there at the bottom of the bed watching this. It was several minutes before she let him go and flopped back on the bed.

'That was just perfect,' she said, licking her lips, looking up at me and saw that I was again fully erect and moved down to the end of the bed and beckoned me closer. I moved and with the opening of her mouth, stuck my cock inside and had her again sucking on me. My hands moved up and held her head as I then face fucked her, cumming quite copiously which surprised me at having that much come out after already having cum not long before.

'Again perfect,' she sighed, her eyes shining as she licked her lips and sat back down next to Richard who began fondling a tit. 'How about something to drink Renard. My mouth's quite dry in spite of the fluid I've just taken in.'

So being the maid as it were, went out of the bedroom and downstairs and made some coffee and took it upstairs to find her fondling Richard's cock and balls as he massaged a breast and both stopped as I walked in with the coffee and poured out three cups and passed them over.

'I would have preferred something stronger Renard, but this will do,' she said as she took some sips. 'Do come and sit down with us. Move Richard and let Renard sit down.' This he did but over into the middle of the bed which only left me the side of the bed on his side. There was silence as we drank our coffee and with mine finished I put the cup on the side table and made to get up.

'No Renard. Lay down next to Richard,' she said, taking the empty cup from his hand and placed it with hers on the table on her side of the bed. 'Now Richard. Play with Renard's cock and let's see it rise up.' My face went a bit red at this as I lay down as Richard sat up and leaned towards me, taking hold of my limp dick and began to rub it with his hand. I saw Vivienne sit up and look over his body as he used his hand to try and raise me up, which to my surprise, it did so.

It then hit me that this was the first time that another man had touched me there and I was getting a thrill at having the experience of this happening. I came up quite hard as his hand kept moving up and down and then again to another surprise was that he shifted his body and bent down and took the head into his mouth.

Boy was it hot and not unlike that of Vivienne's as he used his tongue to excite me even further. Another first for me at having a man suck on my erection and I found that I was enjoying it and it wasn't long before I felt my semen forcing its way up and came with quite some force into that mouth that was clamped on the end of my prick.

I couldn't help but smile at him as he lifted his head up and showed me with his open mouth that he was holding all my sperm inside and watched as he swallowed it with a smile and then licked his lips.

'Nice taste Renard,' he said and I looked down and saw that he now had a massive hard on and saw Vivienne's hand come round to take hold of it.

'This is for me,' she said, giving it a tug as she rolled out of sight but saw her lying back as Richard moved to lay on top of her, watching her legs open for him to move in between them. He rose up onto his knees and I could see his throbbing cock briefly before he lowered himself down and pushed it up into her as her hands came up to his shoulders.

'Lovely,' she crooned as he began to fuck her and I just lay there, surprised at my own calmness in watching him fuck my wife. Both were panting as his bum kept rising up and falling down as his prick moved in and out of her, her legs rising up as I guessed she was reaching her peak.

'Harder, harder,' she gasped and he began really ramming himself into her and saw his back bend slightly as he became rigid and only his hips were moving as he came up on extended arms to cum himself inside her. There were grunts from both of them as he came and she began to buck underneath him as she had her orgasm, giving out a cry as she came.

Her legs then dropped down as he slumped forward, squashing her breasts as I saw him heaving and panting away for a few minutes before rising up and pulling out to roll towards me and saw his shiny cock lay up on his stomach. It fascinated me at seeing this still hard cock that had been up inside my wife, covered in her juices and had this sudden urge to taste it myself and without really knowing what I was doing, had risen up onto my side and bent my head down and began to lick his cock.

What a thrill ran through me at doing this and wanted even more and so lifted it up with my hand and took the head into my mouth to suck it. My heart was thumping away in my chest as my mind had gone berserk at there was me, a bank manager married to the most beautiful woman I had ever seen and yet here I was, sucking on another man's cock. Christ! Even my own body was responding to this by having my own cock rise up again as I sucked on the cock in my hand.

I was tasting the fluids of my wife and I'm sure that I was getting some of his sperm too as I sucked and gently chewed on the head as I squeezed it and kept on sucking and licking. I felt his hand come onto my head and give it some strokes as my head was bobbing up and down on what I had in my mouth.

I finally released him and sat up, feeling somewhat proud at what I had just done, something I'd never dreamed I would ever do and then realized that my wife was looking at me and suddenly felt a bit ashamed at having had her see me suck on another man's cock and felt my face go all red.

I couldn't get off the bed quick enough and fled the bedroom and went into the spare room and into the bathroom there and looked at myself in the mirror. My mind was in a turmoil at what I had just done, sucking on another man that had just fucked my wife and I had watched and hadn't tried to stop him from doing this. You couldn't have done it, my mind said. He's much bigger than you and would make mincemeat of you, which I had to admit was true.

My cock was still up and throbbing at what I had done and so stripped off that underwear and went into the shower and turned the valve to cold and had this spray over me to try and calm myself down which did the trick at making my erection dissipate. Back to my normal state, I dried myself off and collected the underwear which I had strewn around the bathroom and put it away and dressed in my usual clothes I went downstairs and poured myself out a strong drink to steady my shattered nerves.

I don't know how long I was down there but know that I was on my third drink when Vivienne came into the room wearing a dressing gown.

'There you are! You rushed out without a word after sucking on Richard. Why?' she asked, coming over and taking a sip of my drink.

'I…I felt ashamed at you seeing me do that. I can't believe I did what I did,' I said, shaking my head, trying to get the thought to leave my mind.

'There's no reason to feel ashamed. I felt quite proud of you doing it and it even gave me a thrill at seeing you do it,' she said, finishing my drink and going and pouring out another, passing the glass to me.

'Where's Richard now?' I asked.

'Oh, gone. Everything seemed to die after you left, so it was just a kiss he gave me before getting dressed and leaving. It had been so exciting having you see me having sex with another man that we should do it more often.'

'No, we can't. I've got to go back to work tomorrow,' I said, which I did, not asking her if she would be having him come around while I was there. I didn't want to know in case she had said yes.

I HAD to have a taxi take me to the bank next day for on going to the hospital, I had left the Bentley at the bank. On arrival, I had members of the staff ask after my hand and said they were pleased to see me back, though I think from some, it was said with tongue in cheek. There was little that I missed in being away for that short time and it was back to the normal day in quick order.

On returning home that evening, Vivienne made no mention of Richard calling that day and I didn't ask and it seemed that the previous day had been like a dream to me for she never mentioned that either. As usual, on Saturday morning, she played the part of the maid in bringing me my breakfast in bed where after, we had sex which I enjoyed, but then couldn't get out of my mind that I was sticking my erection up into the same place that Richard had as I fucked her.

I groaned afterwards when she reminded me that I had promised her father that I would attend the home game of his football team, to which we duly went. She went to every match both home and away and it was then that I remembered that when the away match was far from home, the team stayed overnight as she did. So this must be when she became attached to Richard at these away games though I learned later that it was not only him she slept and had sex with.

So that afternoon we sat in the directors box to watch the game and had drinks with her father during half time and in the second half, was secretly pleased when Richard, playing right back, brought down an opposing player in the box and got a red card and was sent off. They scored with the penalty and so the home team lost by this one goal. We stayed for an early dinner with her father, commiserating with him about the lost game and were home quite early and also early to bed for me to go down on Vivienne several times to give her an orgasm and even had her suck on me and take my seed that way. This brought to my mind taking Richard's cock into my mouth and sucking on it, and found that having this thought in my mind brought my cock to feel even harder than I'd ever felt before.

Sunday was my day to play Renard, dressing up and getting an erotic thrill in putting this underwear on and still had an erection when I took in her breakfast. It was quite obvious with it pushing the front of the dress out, which Vivienne noticed, straight away and took the tray from me and put it to one side. Slipped out of bed, put her head up under the dress and sucked me off till I came.

'Do you know,' she said when she came out from under, 'you have a better cock than Richard and taste nicer too.' I was quite pleased in one way by being better, but not in the fact that she had been able to compare us, at least she didn't mention anybody else which I supposed I should be thankful for.

I HAD been back to work for a month since the small accident to my hand when I had the summons to present myself at the Head Office the following day at eleven. Wondering what was afoot, was there on time and taken up to the board room with most of the directors there, with my father-in-law at the head of the table.

I was greeted with a handshake by him, getting up and meeting me halfway into the room. 'Glad you're on time Raymond. You know the rest of them,' he said, waving his hand towards the others seated. 'Take a seat will you,' guiding me to a vacant chair before taking his place. 'We've called you here because of Graham Styles' death last week. We have a vacancy on the board here; and after voting, your name came top. Would you accept this prestigious position of being a member?'

I was gob smacked! Me, a director of the bank? It was all managers dream to reach that valued position and here it was, being offered to me when I was the youngest bank manager that they had.

'We decided that we needed a younger man than us old fogies to give us an insight to what the younger generation really wants from banking,' he added while I was still trying to get my mind into the right gear.

'I...I thank you all for this...this honour. I would like to thank all those who voted for me and offer my apologies for those who didn't, and would gladly accept this...this honour you are bestowing on me and one which I gratefully accept,' I said, giving my answer. Most of them clapped their hands and Sir Eugene had a big smile on his face as he stood up and came round and shook my hand.

'Well said my boy, well said,' he said to me before turning to the others. 'Let's retire to the dining room for a drink before lunch,' he said and guided me to this hallowed hall where I was toasted with their drinks before sitting down for an excellent meal.

It was after the meal, after shaking hands with all the others, they began to leave with me being left along with my Chairman.

'I think you realise Raymond, son, that I pushed for you into this post for I expect you to always vote the same as me.'

'That I will do sir and you can rely on me to support you all the way,' I said, knowing that it was blackmail but I would then be at least trebling my salary and only had to attend the monthly meetings and any odd ones that may be called and not have the daily grind of just being a manager. Won't Vivienne be pleased at this promotion, and couldn't wait to leave to go home and tell her.

It wasn't long before I was driving home to Windsor and after parking the car, went indoors. She must have heard the car on the gravel drive and certainly the shutting of the front door, for she called down to me.

'Renard? Can you bring up some drinks please. Three glasses.'

Three? Richard again? It must be with me coming home earlier than when the bank closes. I got an erotic thrill and an erection because of it, at seeing him fuck Vivienne and then me sucking on his cock again. Now where did that last thought came from? I wondered, thinking of his cock? Shaking my head and try to clear these images. I went upstairs and got out the underwear before stripping off my outer clothes. Having a slight problem of getting the underpants off because of this erection. I then put on a pair of black silk panties to keep my erection from showing later. I got that thrill again, run up and down my spine like a tingle as I put the underwear on. Left off the dress this time but used the wig with the little cap on top.

I went back downstairs and poured out three drinks with them on a tray. Went back upstairs and into the bedroom, again nearly dropping it when I saw that it wasn't Richard but another strange man looking back at me from the bed.

'Renard. Meet Terry,' Vivienne said with a smile, showing no apparent shame at me coming home early again and finding her in bed with another man.

'Well he's not John Terry or Terry Venerables,' I said. Standing just inside the bedroom, dressed as I was meeting this stranger. She gave out a laugh.

'No, silly. It's Terry Jones,' she said.

'Left back?' I sarcastically asked.

'No, he's the goalkeeper,' she said.

I said to myself, *I know of another way of stopping balls*, thinking of emasculating him with my bare hand.

'Nice to meet you Renard,' he said with a smile. I noticed that he was looking at what I had squashed inside the panties more than looking me in the eye.'

'The pleasure's all yours,' I said in a sulky tone of voice.

'Now don't be petulant Renard,' said Vivienne, 'know your place.'

'I know my place and it's where he's lying at the moment,' I said.

'That's no problem. Move over Terry and let Renard get on,' she said, moving herself over a little and with both of us moving so that Terry was in the middle of the bed. The sheet that had been covering his lower half had moved down a way and I saw that he had an erection and it looked as big and yet a little better than that of Richard. My mouth went dry at the sight and now lost all petulance as I wanted to get closer to it. So I put the tray down on the side and got onto the bed next to him.

I had butterflies in my stomach as I saw it lying on his stomach. It was an effort to tear my eyes away to reach the glasses and give them one each. They both sat up to drink. Vivienne's breasts shimmering with the movement and Terry's cock now stood out at an angle as they took the offered drinks.

'Take those panties off, Renard. You look quite uncomfortable in them. Let Terry see what you've got for he likes men like you as well as women like me,' Vivienne said after taking a sip of her drink.

Now what did she mean exactly in what she had said. Terry likes men like me? The only thought that came to mind was that he must be bi-sexual which proved to be the case a short while later.

'You do rather have a nice cock,' said Terry, giving my erection a stroke after me having taken off the panties.

'So have you Terry,' said Vivienne, now stroking his, 'and I would like you to use it inside me.' Terry seemed to give out a sigh as he passed me his glass and rolled onto his side towards Vivienne. She had already put her glass down and pulled him on top of her as she moved down the bed a little to be flat on her back. Turning back, I saw him lying there on top of her, squashing her big tits before lifting himself up onto his elbows and moving in between her legs that had opened.

I saw his erection bouncing up and down as he did so and then saw it disappear as he lowered his body and moved up a little, knowing that his cock was now sliding up into her. I had a pang of jealousy as he began to fuck her and yet got a vicarious thrill at seeing this other lover of hers reaming the woman who was my wife. Her legs moved up and her heels went over his waist as she began to groan and move under him as he bounced about on top.

'Harder, harder,' she panted. Her hips starting to buck upwards as he began to move faster. His bum cheeks tensing and I couldn't help myself leaning up and stroking them as they moved under my hand. I could feel the muscles there as Vivienne gave out a little scream as she had her orgasm, and felt Terry's bum cheeks tighten with the hard thrusts he was giving her as he came at the same time.

I knew when he'd finished giving her his seed for the cheeks of his bum slackened and his body movements came to a standstill. He too was panting now and knew that he'd used a lot of energy in his fucking of her. He gave out a groan and began to lift himself up and I heard the small sucking noise as he pulled out and I moved back a little as he rolled over her leg to lie flat on his back. His cock, still erect and hard, flopping onto his stomach, shining with the juices of Vivienne.

'Suck on him Renard,' said Vivienne, raising herself up onto an elbow as she looked over at me. 'I want to watch as you do it.'

I took my eyes off that still throbbing cock that was twitching as it lay there and looked up to see Terry smiling. 'Suck it!' was the order from Vivienne, and being the dutiful husband that I am, tentatively put my hand onto his cock and lifted it up and got a thrill run through my body as I felt the heat and pulse beat of it. I gave my lips a lick and moved down a little and bent over his thigh as I opened my mouth and took the head into it.

I had closed my eyes and got another tingle run up and down my spine as I sucked some of her juices off the head and began to use my tongue over the bare hard flesh, the foreskin having been pushed right down. What I didn't know was that Vivienne had the camera on her side of the bed and took a picture of me as I sucked on Terry's erection. This I saw later and was most mortified for my face was clearly seen to be sucking on another man's cock. But I didn't know this at the time and was having a lovely glow in my gut as I sucked and gently chewed on this organ.

I had sucked him clean and lifted my head up and gave the head of his cock a kiss before letting go and laying back myself, licking my hand of the other juices that had been down on the shaft that I had been holding.

'Now you suck on him Terry for I think he needs the release now,' she said, which I did, for my cock was now really throbbing and it was beginning to hurt. He didn't need any urging from either of us for he was quick to move himself down the bed and I gave out a shiver as he took my erection into a firm grip in his hand as he lifted it upright.

He smiled up at me as his mouth opened and turned his head and bent down and I had him take the head of my cock into the hot interior of his mouth. I gave out a shudder as I felt him move my foreskin down and then had his tongue excite me as it stroked itself over the G string.

God, I was in heaven as I felt the suction of his mouth as his hand moved up and down, sliding the skin over the hard muscle and knew that it wouldn't be long before I came. It was then that I saw the camera in Vivienne's hand and that she took a picture of this man sucking on me. There was a pang of annoyance at her doing this but my mind quickly went back to the pleasure I was getting and began to buck my hips a little as I felt the first surge of my semen begin its journey up from my balls and had the relief as it spurted into his mouth, easing the pressure from my balls as more followed until he had it all.

He had stopped sucking as his mouth began to be filled with my sperm and now that I had finished cumming, felt the suction as he then swallowed it all. God it was lovely and knew that he was a better cock sucker than Vivienne as I tried to compare the different techniques that they both used in this act of oral sex. The air seemed cold as it wafted around the head of my cock as he lifted his head up, releasing me from the heat of his mouth.

'Pure essence Renard. Really lovely,' he said, smiling, still rubbing my cock gently that was already starting to lose its hardness. 'Will you fuck me with it later?'

Wow! That was like a bullet between the eyes. He wanted me to fuck him? I couldn't get my brain around this request and didn't know what to say.

'Now that I would like to see,' Vivienne chipped in. 'I've never seen one man fucking another, but till he's ready Terry, you can suck on me now.' Terry gave out a sigh and a smile up at me as he let go of my prick that had suddenly gone hard again, to move his body away from me to roll over and get between Vivienne's open legs.

I saw his head moving about as he licked and sucked on her but it wasn't being registered in my mind, for that was now back to the way I had stroked the cheeks of his bum earlier, an impulsive move on my part and was now trying to get my mind on the fact that he wanted me to stick my dick in between them and fuck him.

Could I do it? Would I do it? Did I want to do it? My cock was giving me the answer for it began to throb again and be as hard as it was before he had sucked on it. A shiver ran through my body as I realized that I would fuck him even though it was something that I had never done before or even ever thought of wanting to fuck another man. Would it be the same as having a woman? Would I get the same pleasure from it? Well women like having a male cock up inside them and it seems that some men like it too, so there must be some pleasure in both the giving and receiving of a hard cock being used up in the backside.

But would he then want to fuck me, ay, there's the rub? Then came the questions again. Could I let him stick his cock up into me? Would I let him? Would I enjoy it? Maybe he wouldn't ask which made the other questions quite irrelevant and I was brought back from my musing by having Terry roll up against me as he had finished plating Vivienne and missed and didn't hear her cries as she had another orgasm through his ministrations.

'That was lovely Terry,' she said as she leaned over and kissed him. 'Oh, look! Renard's got a hard on again,' and she turned to her bedside cabinet and out of the drawer, she produced a condom. Now why the hell did she have condoms in that drawer? We'd never used them in our sexual couplings, or, the thought struck me, maybe she had one or more of her lovers fuck her up the backside as a change of venue from having a cock in the normal place for a woman. It was a question that I wasn't going to ask, for what I didn't know wouldn't hurt me. It was bad enough that even though she was married to and had sex with me, she still had other men fuck her, making me a cuckold.

She passed the condom to Terry who tore open the wrapper and held it in his hand as he turned to me.

'Would you like to use this and fuck me? I guarantee that you'll enjoy it. Much tighter and you get more feeling than having a woman,' he said and saw the indecision in my eyes and quickly carried on. 'I think I'm right in thinking that you've never done this before,' to which I nodded. 'I promise you that you will enjoy it. It's done doggie fashion and I would like you very much to give me the pleasure of being your first man for I think that what you've got will give me even more pleasure. Please say yes,' he asked, his eyes betraying the fact that he was in fact pleading with me for the right answer. I still debated whether to or not and wondered if by me doing as he asked would degrade me in Vivienne's eyes. I looked over at her and saw that she was smiling and nodding her head, her eyes shining at the prospect of seeing me fuck another man.

'Go on Renard, you'll like it, besides, I've always wanted to see how two men have sex together, please, for me,' she said. Well as I seemed to do all that she asked of me, gave Terry a nod and had his face break out into a wide smile as he moved down the bed. I had nodded because my mouth had gone so dry that I don't think I could have uttered the simple word yes.

Terry lifted my erection up and bent down and gave the head a quick suck before rolling the condom down over the head and covering the shaft, rather expertly I thought. And looking down at my body saw how ludicrous I looked with this condom clad erection lying up on my stomach, almost touching the suspender belt that was around my waist, and seeing my stocking clad legs as well. I even looked at the bra that was across my chest and thought that I now looked ridiculous but they didn't make any comments on this and wondered if they'd seen all this before.

'There shouldn't be any need to tell you where it goes,' Terry said as he rose up from his roll and got onto his knees with his bum now in the air as he leaned forward to rest himself on his forearms. It was if I was looking at some kind of film from the outside as I saw myself rise up onto my knees and shuffle around to get in between his legs. He moved them further apart and in doing so, the cleft between the cheeks of his bum opened so that I could see the target where I was about to put my condom covered prick.

I put my left hand onto his hip to steady me as I moved in closer, holding my cock in my right hand and had a tremor run through me as I guided it and touched his rear entrance with it. By leaning forward slightly, I could release the hold on myself with my body pressure keeping it there and brought my right hand up to his other hip.

Here we go, I thought as I then leaned my body forward and felt the resistance of his ring as I began pressurizing it to open and looking down saw that the head of my cock was being slightly compressed as it began to move into him. Wow, I thought to myself as I saw it slowly moving up into him and suddenly the head was inside him, being really squeezed now that it was on the inside of his body.

'Wow,' I heard from Vivienne with her seeing it go in as it did, and both of us watched as I felt the rest of my cock slide into the fiery heat of Terry's body. Christ! He was right in it being a tighter fit than a woman and I felt rather comfortable as I came to a stop with my thighs pressed up tight to the cheeks of his bum. Feeling his muscle flexing itself around my cock which made it twitch in response and getting a glow in my balls at being where I'd never been before. In an orifice where the sun never shines, and nearly gave out a girlish giggle at this thought.

But I was there, behind a male and had my cock stuck up his backside to which I then started moving to fuck this tight hole. Tight it was too, around the whole length of the shaft and found it very enjoyable in the sliding of my rampant cock back and forth as I fucked him. But like a quote I once read in a book with the title Magenta, "Time is a fickle thing, misery seems to last forever while joy passes in a flash."

It wasn't misery for me but some form of joy for I found that I was nearly at the point of cumming and so held his hips even tighter and really began to push myself harder up into him, pulling his hips back to my forward thrusts. Then I stared to cum, feeling it swell my cock a bit more as I held his body tight to mine with only my hips jerking away as I began shooting my load into the condom stuck up inside his backside.

What a lovely feeling that was to be having my cock squeezed all the time as I came in several hard thrusts into his rear end before coming to a sudden stop, taking in breath as if I'd just run a mile. I was leaning over his rear end, panting away and heard, as if from a distance, the crooning of Terry beneath me and the small cries of delight from Vivienne.

'From the smile on your face Renard, I think you enjoyed that,' she said, her voice now coming into my ears in the normal sound waves. I could only nod, still not having enough breath in my lungs to answer her, which might have come out as a squeak if I had tried.

'What a lovely fuck,' I heard come from Terry, not being able to see whether he had a smile or not, but it sounded like he had, for all I could see was the back of his head. I could now feel that because of my kneeling position, that I was stretching the suspender straps that were running down my thighs though not quite cutting in to me.

Now having fucked my first man, I began to pull myself back and felt Terry's inner muscle clench itself around my cock as I began to slide out of him and heard him give out a little cry as I came out.

'I didn't hurt you, did I?' I asked solicitously, my hands still on his hips as my still hard cock pointed downwards between my thighs almost touching his balls.

'No, no. It was wonderful. It's just that the pulling out of such a tool that's been giving you pleasure is a loss, that is the worse part of this coupling,' he said. I didn't really appreciate those words of his until later.

Vivienne passed some tissues across to me and I used these to cover the condom and pulled it off my still hard and throbbing cock. I had sat back on my heels as I did this and Terry had moved his legs out of the way as he now turned round, still on his knees and fell forward and quickly took the head of my steaming cock into his mouth to suck with some vigor and found out later, that there is always a small amount of sperm left in the head of the cock and it was this that he was sucking out of me. I then got a big kiss planted on the head when he'd finished his sucking and got another surprise when he rose up. For he pulled me up off of my heels and brought his hands up to my head and kissed me.

This was a bit of a shock, being kissed by another man and was somewhat stunned and unable to stop him in his kissing of my lips. I was collecting firsts like gold medals at an Olympic games! I was still in his embrace when he twisted me round so that we fell on the bed with him still kissing me as he landed on top, feeling that he now had an erection and had it being squashed between our stomachs.

'What a wonderful fuck Renard,' he breathed out when the kissing stopped. 'You're a man above men.' An accolade that I didn't think that my part of what we had just done merited this. 'Was I right? Did you enjoy it?' His eyes shining as he spoke, looking down into mine.

'Yes, I must admit that I did,' which was true. I did enjoy the tightness that I had felt all round my cock as it moved inside him and now not ashamed at enjoying the kisses I got afterwards either.

'Would you like to try and have sex the same way?' he then asked of me. The question that I had dreaded had now been spoken and I felt my face go a bright red to my mind.

'Go on! Say yes,' Vivienne jumped in. 'You'll like it.'

'How would you know?' I asked, leaning my head to one side for Terry was still on top of me.

'Well I've had it. In fact I was having two at the same time. It was great having two cocks sliding about inside me.' This was another shock to me that she, my wife, have had sex with two men at the same time. No doubt with the rest of the football team watching when they played away. Which was exactly what she had been doing, playing away while I was at home on my own for those football away matches.

I was wavering about my answer until she said, 'I'll even give you the thrill of being underneath you, sucking on the erection that you'll get. I know, I've seen it all before, but not with you,' she added on the end of admitting to these adulterous shenanigans. Terry leaned into me and gave me a sweet kiss. 'I'll be gentle and I'm sure you'll enjoy it and as Viv has said, it'll give you a hard on and that she'll suck on you at the same time.'

'You...you're sure it won't hurt,' I stammered, looking up into his eyes.

'It won't and I'll be as gentle as I can,' he said, his eyes appearing to be telling the truth though the proof of the pudding etc. My mind was racing about so much that I couldn't really formulate anything that my brain was trying to tell me, so without having any other form of guidance, took a deep breath and said the one word, yes.

Vivienne clapped her hands and I felt the bed move as she got out another condom as Terry, eyes alight, rolled off to allow me to get up and saw the smiling face of my wife pass over a condom that she had already taken out of its wrapper. He took it and expected him to ask me to give the head of his, what now looked to me as being the biggest thing since the Eiffel Tower, a suck for good luck or something along those lines. But he didn't, and quickly rolled it down over his erection and sat back on his heels waiting for me to assume the right position to be fucked.

This must be how those French aristocrats felt during the revolution as they climbed the steps to the guillotine I thought, my heart thumping away inside my chest, the bra strap now straining with the deep breaths I was trying to take in. Blood was pounding around my body and in my head as I slowly moved, feeling what to me felt like large butterflies hurling themselves around in my stomach.

Getting onto my knees, I looked for the block to rest my neck on for the axe to fall, but saw only the pillow and Vivienne, out of the corner of my eye, moving down the bed for a better view of her husband being fucked up the ass. I started trembling as I felt Terry move in between my legs, nudging them wider apart as he got into position.

'Better use some cream for the first time,' I heard Terry say.

'I'll get some,' she said and felt the bed move as she got off. It seemed an agonizingly long time before she came back with me just having the pillow to stare at. 'Here,' she said. Obviously passing a pot of cream to Terry.

'This'll feel a little bit cold,' he said and I flinched as a blob of this cream was pressed to anoint this foxhole that he was going to delve in. He must have passed the pot back to Vivienne, for a hand came to my hip and I flinched again as if felt what would be the head of his prick press against the entrance to my rear. This caused me to shiver and was still in this state when his other hand came to my other hip.

'Being your first time, it may hurt a little if you don't relax. That's the secret. Relax and don't fight the entry,' Terry said as I felt him lean into me and feel the pressure moving against my ring piece.

Sweat was running down from my forehead and had to shake my head to clear it from my eyes as I felt more pressure being applied to my rear entrance.

'Relax Renard, relax,' said Terry as the pressure got greater and found that the head was enlarging me bigger than any crap I'd ever had. It was starting to hurt me; the bugger lied, my mind was crying out until I got a sudden hard slap on a cheek of my bum that made me jump and at that moment, the head of his cock was inside me, to be followed by the rest of his cock until his thighs were pressed up against the cheeks of my bum.

Christ! It had hurt a little at him trying to get into me but now he was there, all I could feel was the pulsating throb of his erection that was making itself known apart from the size of it filling me as it was. I felt I had nerves there that I didn't know of and had them all giving out different kinds of signals as he began to move and have his cock giving me all funny kinds of sensations in that narrow channel that he was moving in.

My own sphincter muscle was constantly contracting itself involuntarily round his shaft as though to hold it there as he moved, feeling him start to widen the entrance again before sliding forward again till his thighs touched mine. Backwards and forwards he moved and I then began to get a thrill at the feelings that the nerves there inside me were reacting to this intrusion.

I also found that I was drooling at the mouth and was loving this internal massage I was getting and also that my cock was now fully erect and bouncing up and down to Terry's movements in his fucking of me. I flinched when I felt a hand take hold of it and remembered that Vivienne said she would suck on me and saw part of her body alongside of me, not having noticed her moving at all.

How hot her mouth felt as she managed to get the head of my cock in between her teeth and rather rasped it with me being moved about by Terry in his motions of fucking me. God I was now in another kind of heaven at what I was feeling inside me and having my cock sucked at the same time.

I came almost at once at having Vivienne suck on me, feeling my sperm surge up from my balls as she avidly sucked on my throbbing cock. Loving the new and strange ways her teeth were raking me as she took all that I expelled and the sudden release of her mouth as she gave a gasp and a hiccup, which I think was by the swallowing of my sperm.

Now Terry started to move a bit faster, his fingers digging into my hips and being pulled backward to his forward thrusts and then start to feel his balls slapping the lower cheeks of my bum. His thrusts were harder and I was really being rocked on my knees by his fast moving, knowing that he was about to cum and shoot his load inside me, making me wonder what it would feel like if he wasn't wearing a condom. Now he held me tight to his thighs and had his cock throb even more inside me and it felt as if it expanded a little bit more as I knew that he was then actually cumming inside me.

He came to a sudden stop and I had his full weight lean over my rear end, his cock really now throbbing away inside me, his breath sounding very loud as he panted, almost as if he were gasping for breath. I found I was panting too and was marveling at the thrill I was getting at having him inside like he was.

His weight lifted up off of me and felt his cock starting to slide out, my sphincter muscle of its own accord, was gripping his shaft as much as it could though to no avail and felt my ring being expanded again to a little pain as it finally left my backside. I couldn't help but give out a little cry at this sudden loss of being and having my insides thrilled in such a way. Feeling much the same as a child having its favorite toy taken away from him, so much that I could have cried at the removal of that wonderful cock that had just reamed me. I had the fleeting thought of why had I hesitated when first asked if he could fuck me. Now having had it once, there would be no hesitation to saying yes if the question was ever asked again.

I felt like a limp rag with his removal from fucking me and fell forward onto my front, not even having the energy to roll over. But with my head to one side, saw Vivienne move with tissues in her hand, strip the condom off Terry's still outstanding erection and take the head of this into her mouth to suck out any residue that was still there.

Finishing this, she turned her smiling face to me as she flopped down, her face inches away from mine on the pillow.

'How was it?' she asked.

'Incredible,' I croaked out.

'But did you enjoy it?'

'Yes, I did,' I admitted, which was true. Loathe that I had been at the first, but they had been right and it was enjoyable in spite of the pain at the entry of his cock into me. What had followed had been terrific in more ways than one, like the thrill of being fucked, my nerves being sent into all kinds of tingling modes and the wonderful new meaning of having a massage.

I rolled onto my back as Terry settled himself down alongside of me and leaned over and kissed me.

'That was truly wonderful Renard. I hope I didn't hurt you too much for I know it can be a little painful at first,' he said.

'Yes there was some pain but other than that, it was worth it,' I said, pulling his head back down to mine for me to then kiss him for the pleasure he had just given me.

Such was the glow inside of me that I paid no attention to what we were talking about to each other for quite some time until it sank in that Terry said it was time for him to go home. I came awake as it were but still retained that euphoria of having sucked and fucked him and had him fuck me and having Vivienne sucking on me at the same time that I even had visions of me fucking him again and also having somebody else fucking me at the same time as I would then also be sucking on another erect penis and really know that I was then in Shangri La.

I idly lay there and watched him get dressed and when ready to leave, came back to the bed and gave Vivienne a kiss as he stroked a breast and then came and gave me one with a stroke of my now limp organ before saying goodbye. I didn't even have the energy to get up and see him out and believe it or not, fell asleep.

IT WAS early evening before we both woke up and feeling hungry and rather thirsty, we got up and as we were, went downstairs to get a drink first before starting to think about dinner. I was still in Renard's underwear and Vivienne naked, so we both put on pinny's as we worked together in preparing dinner. It wasn't until we sat down and in the middle of our meal did I remember as to why I had come home early and so told her that I was now a member of the board of directors of the bank.

'How wonderful!' she cried, jumping up and coming around to give me a hug and a kiss. 'I knew daddy wouldn't let us down,' and went to the fridge and brought out a bottle of champagne, passing to me to open as she got two fresh glasses out. The cork popped out, shooting across the kitchen and managed not to let the drink froth out of the bottle as I filled both glasses.

'To my husband,' she began, raising her glass, 'now a bank director and a most wonderful lover,' and emptied the glass with this toast. I then raised my glass.

'To my wonderful wife and lover of all men,' and quickly downed my glass hoping she didn't pick up on my awful faux pas at what I had just said. Thankfully she didn't and we went on to finish the bottle as well as our dinner and opened another bottle to drink. With that also drunk, we decided to leave the washing up till the morning and with yet a third bottle opened, with this and our glasses, went back up to bed where we finished that before making love and both getting enjoyment with our coupling as well as the cleaning up of our bodies with our tongues.

I WOKE up in the morning with a furry tongue and found that not only had two studs popped out of the stockings, for I had fallen asleep still wearing that female attire, but that I had also laddered one of the stockings.

'That doesn't matter,' she said as I cursed at this ruined stocking. 'I've still got several more pairs, anyway, with the increase in your salary that you will now be getting, a pair of stockings is like a drop in the ocean.' It wasn't the money side that I was thinking of, it was just that one was ruined for I found that I liked wearing this get up and was loathe to stop wearing this decadent female underwear. I was even tempted to wear this under my male clothing but discarded the idea for what would it look like if I had an accident of sorts and was shipped off to hospital. I'd literally be unfrocked in public. It didn't bear thinking about. But at home, well, that was a different matter.

With me now being on the board of directors of our bank, I didn't have to go to work every day like I used to and so got to understand Vivienne because I was bored and so took to having sex every day with her. She devised many scenarios for us to have sex in though most of them was with me being subservient to her wishes, which now, I'm not ashamed to admit, fell into this habit of doing everything she asked of me. Well I think I've already proved that by accepting the fact that I was a cuckold and actually joined in with her lovers, which I found out, she currently had four. This didn't take long to find out as there was a different one once a week and I then got roped in to playing with them too, especially after being presented to them as Renard, all dressed up in the maid's outfit.

Terry, I now knew was bi-sexual. Richard I wasn't too sure of as yet for I'd only briefly sucked on his erection once. The next one was Robert who was definitely heterosexual and didn't want male sex but I still had to be in the bedroom for he didn't mind being watched as he fucked my wife. I was definitely the spare prick when it was his turn to shaft her, just being there with a steaming hard on and not getting to have Vivienne until after he had left. Then I was commanded to go down on her and suck on her, getting quite some semen of Robert in the process as well as her juices that mixed the two together as she had her orgasm. The fourth one, Michael was like Terry in being bi-sexual and here I joined in.

Dressed as Renard, I let him into the house and he really believed that I was a maid until, in the bedroom, I took off the dress which amused him greatly to see that I was a male dressed up in female underwear. At least he didn't laugh when he saw me like this but gave out a low whistle.

'Well that's surprised me Vivienne,' he said. 'I didn't know that you had a transvestite as a lover too.'

'He's not a transvestite for I've made him dress up like this, he's my husband.' At least he had the decency to blush as he looked at me again, standing there in this underwear with my cock already halfway to an erection. I blushed too at Vivienne telling him that I was her husband and felt rather foolish at her doing so.

'Er, does, does he just watch or join in?' Michael asked.

'Both, for I think he now likes having a man too. Well get acquainted then. Renard! Kiss Michael,' she said. With her emphasizing the maid's name, I knew it was an order and so with my face still red, moved over to Michael who was still dressed and took him into my arms and kissed. This act now brought me up to a full erection and on breaking off the kiss, he now looked down at me having felt it as our bodies had come together.

'I like what I felt and can now see,' he said. 'Will you fuck me with it later?'

'Yes later,' Vivienne jumped in. 'I want you first Michael so get those things off,' she said as she took off her gown to reveal her lovely naked body before she got onto the bed. Michael was quick to then get his clothes off to show that he was up and ready with his nice looking cock standing out proud from his groin. At seeing it bounce up and down as he got on the bed made my insides flutter for I now wanted it, both to suck and have it put inside me.

There wasn't any foreplay for he got straight in between her open legs and buried himself inside her. Her legs came up and he began to move in his fucking of her. I watched his backside moving up and down as he humped away and I could see his balls swinging backwards and forwards and moved forward and even took them into my hand. He stopped in mid fuck as he felt me take hold of them, but carried on as he knew I was being gentle in handling them.

They were like soft plums inside their sac and I could feel them move so easily inside and when he started to ejaculate, I felt them move upwards, almost disappearing inside him with every time he was pumping out his sperm cells. I only let go of them when he started to pull out of Vivienne.

'That was lovely as usual Vivienne,' he said as he rolled over onto his back having had his oats, his glistening cock laying up on his stomach.

'I'll let Renard clean you up,' she said, looking at me, turning her head to look at the cock that had just been inside her and knew that that was what she wanted me to do, so I moved closer and got onto the bed between his legs until I was just above his groin, looking down at his lovely looking cock there waiting for me to suck on.

This I did after lifting it upright and taking the wet head into my mouth. I felt him tense up a little as he felt the heat from my mouth close over the head and felt my tongue touch him. It was hot and hard and I could feel it throbbing as I sucked and pulled out a little of his semen from the eye, getting to taste him as well as some of Vivienne's juices. He had given out a groan as I had taken him in and relaxed as I continued to suck and lick all around the head until all of their juices I had cleaned off before lifting up off him, quite pleased at having done what I did and gave the eye of his cock that seemed to wink at me when I squeezed his it, a poke with the tip of my tongue before giving the head a final kiss.

'That was great Renard,' he said, looking down at my smiling face for I had found that it was great too.

'My turn now Renard,' Vivienne said, and so I moved along the end of the bed and moved in between her legs and buried my face into her vagina and began licking and sucking at her. Here I got some more of his semen that was slowly seeping out of her vagina with her own orgasmic juices until she too was nice and clean again. 'Lovely Renard,' she said when I surfaced. 'Now get onto the bed here,' patting the bed between her and Michael, 'for I'm sure that Michael would like to taste you too.'

I crawled up onto the bed between them, feeling my throbbing erection swaying beneath me as I did so and then turned and lay down on my back. I turned my head to Michael and saw him smiling at me as he rose up and gave me a kiss on the lips before moving down the bed and felt his hand take hold of me and hold it upright.

Like him, I gave out a gasp at feeling the heat as his mouth took in the head of my cock and felt the foreskin being pushed down and had his tongue start to move over the bare flesh, making me tingle when he caught the G spot. His hand was moving up and down in a firm grasp as he started to suck and gently chew on me and such was my need for relief, soon began to buck my hips up to him and started filling his mouth with my seed. It was at least five spurts that came out and I had him then sucking the rest out until I felt that my tanks were dry. But he carried on for a few more minutes in his rubbing and sucking of me before he lifted up from me and gave me a nice smile, letting me see that he still had my semen inside his mouth before he then swallowed it all.

'Now let me see him fuck you Renard,' Vivienne said, 'for it you react like you did with Terry, you'll be up and hard again to fuck him afterwards.' I felt my face go red at her telling him that I'd already been fucked by another man. It was bad enough at having to perform while wearing female underwear, but with the look on her face, did as I was told. He moved for me to roll over onto my front and get up onto my knees as she passed over a condom to him. I didn't see him roll it down on his erection for I was looking at Vivienne's face and saw the sparkling gleam in her eye and believed that seeing me being fucked by another man, turned her on. I must admit, that after being fucked by Terry and the thrill I got from having his throbbing erection up inside me, made me not give any objections to have Michael fuck me and hoping that the experience would be just as exciting.

But I still trembled, having butterflies again in my stomach at the expectancy of having Michael's cock pushed up into me and flinched as I felt his hand steady himself as he got between my open legs behind me.

'Remember to relax yourself Renard,' Vivienne said, moving down the bed a little to watch as this cock was going to be pushed up into my backside. My body gave a little jump as I felt the head of his condom clad erection touch the entrance and my sphincter muscle automatically clenched itself as he kept it there and his other hand came onto my other hip.

'Relax Renard, relax,' she repeated and I tried my best as I felt him lean into me and had the head of his cock push against the resistance he was getting from this clenched muscle. No cream, my mind cried out as he began to win the battle and felt the pain as his cock widened me enough to fully enter. I gave out a small cry at this but then felt the pain start to disappear as I felt the rest of his cock sliding up into me.

'Aaaah,' I breathed out as he slid in, massaging that pain away as his thighs came up against the cheeks of my bum, feeling his cock throbbing away inside and giving me little tingles through the nerves that were there. The backward and forward motions of his cock sliding in me was a balm at ironing out any kinks inside and began to drool at the pleasure his erection was giving me. I even moved the top half of my body down to the bed, bending my spine which brought my bum up higher for him to be able to drive himself even further inside as he fucked me.

It's hard to describe all the emotions that coursed around my body as it rocked to his movements behind me. God, I was loving this internal massage, feeling my own cock starting to rise again as my balls swung back and forth, agitating the sperm cells inside them. The nerves inside my channel were sending out little electric type shocks into my nervous system that in turn affected my glands, hence my drooling at having the pleasure of this hard cock reaming me out.

The fingers of his hands began to tighten themselves on my hips as he began to pull me back to his forward thrusts, feeling his thighs start to really smack up against my bum cheeks and then was held most firmly as his cock swelled a little more and was sure I felt his seed being pumped out from the head of his cock into the condom. What a thrill that was too.

He came to a stop and heard his heavy breathing as his weight started to come down onto my rear end and I had to straighten up so as not to collapse. Even though he had just cum, his cock was still throbbing away and my muscle kept contracting itself at this intrusive piece of flesh that I had and was still giving me pleasure just by being where it was. But as I've said before, joy is but a fleeting moment and tried hard to hold back a sob as he started to pull back out of me, my muscle also now, having failed to prevent the entry, was now trying to stop the removal but again could not stop him leaving my backside for me to feel cold air waft around my shrinking ring piece.

I was almost crying as I fell forward onto the bed and it was Vivienne who stripped off his condom and when I turned my head, saw her sucking on him. I managed to get my leg out from under her without kicking her under the chin as she saw to cleaning up the head of his cock, and rolled over onto my back.

She kept on sucking and licking him till he started to deflate before lifting her head up off with a big smile on her face as she licked her lips.

'Now you,' she said to me. 'Move down the bed a bit,' which I did, guessing what she wanted and I wasn't wrong when she swung a leg across my chest and presented me with her wet fanny just above my face. I just had time to get my hands up on the inside of her thighs as she lowered herself down for me to use my tongue inside her as she took hold of my erect cock. As she took the head into her mouth, her body came right down and it was only my hands that stopped her from smothering me as she began to suck and chew on me and I began to lick and tease her with my tongue.

Such had been the agitation of my balls, the sperm was raring to be let loose and it wasn't long before my hips started to buck and send them out to be swallowed instead of fertilizing her meadow. Also, with me rasping her clit the way I was and probably the taking in of my sperm, she shook and had her orgasm, letting me get her juices come down to my mouth and run down my chin. I was still slurping away when she'd finished licking the head of my cock clean before she lifted herself up off of me and rolled over onto her side.

I sat up to see Michael smiling at me and was a little surprised when he moved over and taking hold of my head and kissing me. Not only kisses but used his tongue to lick my chin, taking some of Vivienne's juices to transfer into his own mouth.

'Okay Michael,' Vivienne began, 'now let's get you ready to fuck me.'

I looked down at his groin and wondered how he was going to fuck her with his cock in the state it was, hanging limply from his groin. I was about to find out as Vivienne got off the bed and went to one of the lower drawers of her tall boy and was surprised to see her turn around with a leather strap in one hand and some thongs in the other.

Now I haven't told you that our bed is of the divan style by not having an end piece but it did have what could be called the headboard, only it wasn't board or of wood but brass. It was of the old antique style by having two big uprights on either side with knobs on top and rails going across between them and several thin ones that went from a lower bar to the main one crossing at the top.

I watched as she took one of Michael's hands first and tied one thong to his wrist before doing the same to the other before he got onto the bed, on his knees and shuffled up closer to this headboard. Vivienne then took the end of the thong and pulled his arm up close to the top rail going across and tied this thong to it and moved over and tied the other one to it too.

I now knew what was going to happen seeing Michael now up on his knees and having his outstretched arms tied to the brass rail, that she was going to belt him across the ass with the leather strap. She was standing by the side of the bed with me sitting, or rather, half lying down on the other, watched as she swung the belt and could almost feel the impact as it struck him across the pale white cheeks of his bum. It landed with a loud crack and his body jumped and he gave out a low moan and saw that he now had a red weal across both cheeks. I was flinching as well as more and more times she swung this strap, adding more weal's to his backside and though he was giving out dry sobs, I saw that his cock was now up and looked even harder than when he used it in me.

It must have been about a dozen lashes that he had across his bum which was now a bright red in color, but his cock looked massive. She quickly untied these thongs for him to move back down the bed for her to get on and lay on her back with her legs either side of those he was kneeling on.

I moved down the bed as she got on and as she opened her arms to him, I saw him fall on her as his massive erect cock went straight up into her and they both gave out a gasp as their groins collided, his chest landing on her tits. Then he raised himself up onto his elbows without moving his lower half before he then started to fuck her.

I was amazed as I watched his red bum, the color now of a bright red apple move up and down as he fucked away, that by using a belt like she had, could cause a man to get an erection like he now had. He must have got some enjoyment out of it to have suffered those blows or was it just to make his cock that much bigger just for her pleasure. I couldn't guess and she soon was bucking herself up to him as she gave out a scream at having her orgasm, almost dislodging him from where he was.

Both were gasping for breath when they came to a stop, both chests heaving, hers being more apparent and it seemed to be an effort for him to rise up and pull out of her. She gave out a cry as he did so, and he rolled over onto his back by my side and I saw that his cock was still in this massive state, shining with her juices.

I couldn't stop myself from quickly moving down the bed and lifting up his cock, feeling that it was still hard and definitely bigger than it had been before. The foreskin had been pushed right back and the head of his cock was a shiny red as the cheeks of his bum, almost glowing like a fire engine's beacon.

It was only this brief look I gave it before taking that lovely shiny cock head into my mouth and knew that it was bigger as my lips closed around it and began to suck on him. I got both his sperm and her juices that was like having a drink and then nearly choked at the thought that with him being gay, was I drinking a fruit cocktail? But I controlled myself and really loved sucking on this wonderful piece of hard flesh I had in my hand and mouth.

I think Vivienne was a bit miffed at me getting to his wet prick first, but tough, I was enjoying having him in my mouth as I sucked and chewed on him in the cleaning up of this cock, now losing some of its hardness. I took it out of my mouth and looked at it, being still red and quite firm in my hand, but now looking as it had been when he had fucked me with it. I made him give out a shiver when I squeezed the head, making the eye open and blew it before sticking the tip of my tongue into it, not really going in of course, but you know what I mean.

I now nibbled my way down the underside of the shaft with him lying on his back, the underside was now at the top. I nibbled down till I got to where his cock disappeared into his body and then had his balls just below my eyes. Moving down a bit more, I was then able to take his ball sac into my mouth and had the pleasure of being able to gently move them about but got a better idea of them by only having one ball there, feeling the softness of this marvel of nature.

Which it is if you think about it would be. Though when you have the male orgasm contents in your mouth, it feels like half a bucket full when it is only around a teaspoon full. Now in this one emission can be anything from two to three million sperm inside and it takes a powerful microscope to be able to see them separately. Then consider that just one of these microscopic life giving organisms is carrying thousands of genes of the person that it comes from. How in hell can this small item hold so much? It's really unbelievable but it's true! Plus the fact that I now found them nice to taste whereas a few months ago wouldn't have dreamed that I would, now liking the way of getting them too.

'As much as I have enjoyed myself, Vivienne and Renard, time flies and it was time I was going,' he said a few minutes later, giving Vivienne a kiss and then one for me, my eyes going slightly wide at feeling the tip of his tongue press against my lips. He pulled away with a smile on his face and I watched him move and get off the bed, his cock swinging nicely by this action and watched it disappear as he pulled his trousers up. When fully dressed, he gave us both a little wave of his hand. 'I'll see myself out, bye,' and he was gone.

We lay there together in silence for quite a few minutes with Vivienne's hand slowly moving over my flaccid cock before she spoke. 'I think you enjoyed our session with Michael, yes?'

'Yes,' having to admit that I had indeed enjoyed it and felt my cock starting to get hard again as I thought back as to how wonderful it had been in not only sucking on his erection but also having had him fuck me. I knew by admitting this to myself that I was now bi-sexual and wouldn't mind having him again in spite of the fact that he also fucked my wife.

I had first felt shocked and belittled when I first found out that I was a cuckold with her taking on a lover, but now having joined in into a threesome, I now wanted them myself so did that make me an adulterer? How can that be, my little voice said, adultery is when a man has sex with another woman other than his wife. I don't know if having sex with another man comes under that banner, I said to myself adding more confusion to my mind.

With having these carnal thoughts as she rubbed my ever growing cock, it came up to being a solid bar of flesh.

'You are a big man Raymond,' making me wonder at the change of name seeing as I was still wearing the maid's underwear and not calling me Renard. 'I can't help myself in wanting an erection like this inside me nearly all of the time, like now. Fuck me Raymond, fuck me and give me another orgasm.'

I couldn't refuse because I wanted to as my cock was now really throbbing and so I moved and got between her legs that opened for me to slide up into her, which I did. The only trouble now as I moved up inside was to compare the difference of sticking my cock into her and pushing it into a man's backside, loving the tightness of a man as compared to the slackness of a woman even though she could contract her vagina somewhat but not be as strong as the one on the inside of a man's rear channel.

But it was still a foxhole to fuck and got on with moving myself inside her and did bring her up to her orgasm, having her buck beneath me as I came at the same time. Both of us had heaving chests when we came to a stop, her breasts glistening with a thin film of sweat that covered them and her eyes shining at her release and a smile on her face. Her mouth puckered up as she felt me start to pull out and gave out a little cry as my cock left her body and I rolled over onto my back, my wet cock slapping down onto my lower stomach.

She was quick to rise up and lean over my side, lifting it up and take the head into her hot mouth and begin to suck out any residue of sperm still inside it. Now the only difference to her sucking on me and that of man was only in the way that the tongue was used as both did much the same and it was nice to be lying down on my back and having this done to me.

I could hear her giving out a moan as my cock was deflating and she was being able to take more of my cock inside until it was all in her mouth with her nose pressed down against my thigh and finally lifted her head for my cock to flop to one side.

'Come on Renard,' she began as she gave a twang to the suspender strap, 'make it rise up to fuck me again.'

'I can't,' I said.

'Well I can if we do what I did with Michael,' she answered.

'What? Use the belt on me?' I exclaimed, raising my head up to see the look of determination on her face.

'Not as many and not as hard Renard. It worked with Michael so why wouldn't it work with you,' she said.

'No!' I cried and she then grabbed my balls and gave them a squeeze.

'Please Renard. You'll enjoy it I promise,' her hand tightening a little more round my balls, the pressure increasing the longer I took to reply until I had to give in.

'Okay, okay, Vivienne. Stop crushing my balls,' I cried and felt some relief when she let go of me and moved off the bed to pick up the thongs and took hold of my wrist.

'No!' I cried.

'Yes,' she said, slipping it over my wrist and pulling it tight and reached over and grabbed my other hand and slipped the other thong over it to tighten it like the other. 'Now turn around on the bed and get up onto your knees.' There was a steely edge to her voice and so I obeyed and slowly with some misgivings, did as she commanded and let her tie my wrists to the top rail of the bedstead.

I began to tremble as I saw her pick up the strap and stand next to the bed and as she raised up her arm, I closed my eyes and really gave a jump and a cry as it came and slashed across my bare backside. Tears came to my eyes and I jumped again at the second swipe and felt the cheeks of my bum burning as she gave me another four strokes of the leather strap and I was actually sobbing at having this done to me. But I then felt that my cock was at a full erection and had been bouncing up and down as I was strapped and it was really throbbing now, but she hadn't finished with me yet.

'As you now like having a man fuck you, now you can have me fucking you,' she said and I turned my head and gave out a gasp for she was in the process of strapping a dildo onto herself.

'No!' I cried, shaking the brass headboard as I tugged at the thongs holding me there.

'Don't be a woose,' she said as she finished strapping it and saw it bounce, just like a man's as she moved over towards me. 'It's the smallest one I've got and there's not much difference from a real live one.' I still had my face turned towards her, my eyes on that swaying piece of rubber that came close up to my face and had it prodded at my mouth. 'Suck on it and give it some lubrication.' I had clenched my jaw at it touching my lips and my mind was raving but came to realize that if I didn't do as she asked I would be getting it anyway and if there wasn't any form of lubrication on it, it was going to hurt.

It was of a dull brown in color and was the exact replica of a circumcised cock in both shape and size of an average man, so rather than have that pain of entry, opened my mouth and had her move it in between my parted lips. At least she didn't push it too far to choke me, just the head and it almost felt like the real thing except that it was not hot and throbbing or had the sort of elasticity of a real cock but slightly on the solid side, just like a dog's rubber bone.

I got as much of my saliva that I could into my mouth to coat this rubber head of the dildo as it was gently moved back and forth inside.

'Okay, open your mouth for we don't want to wipe off the saliva,' she said and so I did as she said and had it removed and saw that the head of this thing was now shiny, and it disappeared from my sight as she moved back and felt the bed dip as she got behind me.

My body was really trembling now and instead of being held on the bed by the thongs round my wrists, I grabbed hold of the rail and saw my knuckles go white as I gripped it as hard as I could, having the premonition that it was going to be a quite painful entry into my backside.

My legs had been pushed open wider by her knees and had a hand hold my hip and also had the suspender straps straining against my thighs and then flinched when I felt this thing touch my ring piece.

'Relax Renard, relax,' she said, 'Just as you've been told to do,' as I felt the pressure starting to build up as she leaned in towards me. I wasn't prepared for the sudden sharp slap that she gave to a bum cheek, making me jump and yet, at the same time made my sphincter muscle relax and the head of this dildo suddenly slipped inside me.

'Christ!' I cried out, for it wasn't exactly a smooth entry. 'That hurt!' but this pain at the expansion of my backside began to quickly subside as I felt the shaft of this rubber cock move further into me, touching parts that I hadn't felt touched before, until her thighs were up against my bum cheeks. The major difference was soon apparent as my muscle kept flexing itself against this intrusion and that was the lack of heat, the pulsation and throb of a real cock. It had little knobbly bits all along its length which I saw later, that gently rasped the insides as she moved in her fucking of me with one of her toys.

The only time it hurt, apart from the initial entry, was when she moved herself backwards but at an angle making its head press more to one side than the other with these little rubber bits pressing harder to the side of my canal.

'I haven't used this for a long time,' she said, moving herself inside me with this rubber cock. 'Also it's now the first time that I can say that I've fucked you instead of you fucking me all the time.'

'And the others,' I gasped at the last few words she had said, referring to her other lovers and grunted at a more violent shove into me at this comment of mine. 'I can't take much more of this,' I cried. 'The lubrication's gone and it's starting to hurt.'

'Then imagine that I'm just about to come inside you,' she said as she began moving quicker with shorter and sharp stabs at me until I felt her hips straining against the cheeks of my bum and felt the cock move up and down a bit as she tried to simulate a man as he shot his load until she came to a stop and leaned over my rear end.

I was almost sobbing and glad that she had come to a halt and then felt her lift off and have it slowly slide back and gave out a cry as I was widened again as the head slipped out. What a relief that was as my ring began to pucker up as it closed up, back into its normal watertight condition.

She wasn't quite finished with me as I felt her get off the bed and saw her undo the straps of the dildo that had been up my backside, seeing the little knobs that had rasped the interior. She let it drop to the floor as she opened the bedside drawer and pulled out a condom. She got it out of its wrapper and moved under me and had her take the head of my now, really throbbing erection and gave me a suck. Just a couple before letting me go and had her then roll the rubber down over the head and smoothed it down the rest of the shaft.

'Now that I've fucked you up the backside,' she began as she started undoing the thongs from the brass rail, 'you can fuck me the same way.' I couldn't believe my ears as I rubbed my free wrists. She wanted anal sex from me? Another first and it wasn't one that I was going to avoid and so I moved over and let her get onto the bed and position herself on her knees. 'How did you like having my little toy?'

'It bloody well hurt,' I said as I moved round behind her and got in between her open legs. 'It hurt like this,' I said as I suddenly grabbed her hips and rammed my cock straight up her ass. I was pleased to hear the cry that she gave out at my forceful entry but was then annoyed when she said that she only cried out at the force I had used, not of the entry because she hadn't had time to use the muscle to try and prevent the moving into her.

But I was there now with my throbbing fit to bust cock, well inside and really gave her a real right reaming, pulling her back onto me as I thrust forward and even though it had only been a short while before that I had already cum, I didn't last as long as I would have liked in fucking her backside and came in ragged bursts to send my sperm into the condom.

I was puffing like a train as I came to a halt, leaning over her back, feeling the sweat running down my chest. Different as it had been, I was not going to let her tie me up again and use that bloody dildo again on me, but I wouldn't mind fucking her up the bum another time. Which happened in the following week that we'll come to in a minute. We stayed naked for the rest of the day, though it wasn't really true for me as I was still wearing the underwear and only added the pinny when helping get dinner, her putting one on too.

It would be another week before I would be required to present myself at the Head Office for the monthly meeting of the board and so with me being at home every and all day, wondered if that as she was now having me fuck her every day, she would give up having these other lovers. But then I realized that I would be cutting my nose off to spite my face if I insisted on this for I had liked sucking on their cocks and having a cock pushed up inside me, so didn't say anything along these lines. Nor did I stop her from going to the away matches with the team as I felt it prudent to stay on her good side and not have her deprive me of the sex I would be getting from her lovers.

The one I wouldn't have minded her getting shot of was Robert, for when he duly turned up the week that it was his turn, I had to watch him fuck Vivienne and he wouldn't let me fuck him nor would he fuck me. The only thing he did allow and that was for me to suck on his cock after he pulled out from fucking my wife which I thought was rather unfair.

Though I did join in as I will tell you. Vivienne wanted to be fucked by both of us at the same time which I thought would be impossible but was soon put right.

I already had an erection that was begging to be seen to after seeing him kissing and fondling the tits that really belonged to me. She made this suggestion and rolled a condom down over my prick and made me lie down on my back. She got astride of me and facing down towards the bottom end of the bed, had her hand down between her legs and held it upright as she nestled the head against her ring piece.

It was only then that the light dawned on me as she let herself down slowly, taking my cock up into her backside, giving out little grunts as she was expanded to fit the head of my cock that disappeared from sight as she sank right down onto my thighs with a big sigh.

I had her full weight on my groin as she straightened her legs out and then leaned back to be laying on top of me with my cock stuck there up her backside. My hands moved up and began to squeeze her tits as I saw Robert move forward, spreading not only my legs but hers too as he moved in towards her, his big erection moving out of sight and then I had another incredible experience.

For as Robert entered her, I could feel the head of his cock slide up along with the shaft, for there is only a membrane separating the two different channels. It was fantastic to have his cock almost rubbing mine as he moved in and then to feel it move backward and forward as he fucked her, moving my cock at the same time. Because of this, I came far too soon, shooting my load up into the condom and only after I have had my release did I feel the weight of the pair of them on my hips. As thrilling as the original feeling had been, it was a little spoiled by having to suffer this weight, but it was still great to have his cock rubbing me as he fucked away and got just as excited as he came, really ramming himself into her as he let go of his seed. He was laying down on her body after cumming and I couldn't help but almost scream at him to lift off.

He must have realized then that I was supporting both of them on my body and he lifted himself up and felt his cock sliding out of her as the pressure came up off of my lower body. With him now out, he helped Vivienne up off of me to my relief and had her pull off the condom and to let me move to take the head of Robert's wet cock into my mouth to suck and felt her take mine into hers with the same purpose in mind. As I said, this was the only sex I could have with him and managed to get Vivienne to dump him and either only have Richard, Terry and Michael or find another bi-sexual lover to take his place, which she did and wasn't at all surprised that it turned out to be another member of her father's football team. Keep it in the family was her answer to the whys and wherefores of this choice.

'Are all the football team bi-sexual, apart from Robert?' I asked her one day.

'No, there's six that I know of and that they sometimes fuck each other when in the pool after a success against another team,' she said. 'Well you've seen the way some of them kiss a goal scorer, sometimes looking as if they were trying to fuck him when he was on his back on the park.' The park being their term for the football pitch.

The new lover of my wife was known as Steve and he just loved seeing me in my underwear and would, when it was his turn to have Vivienne, always had a suck on my erection before moving over and kissing Vivienne before we got down to the nitty gritty of having a threesome. I came to love these four men as much as she did with them becoming my lovers as well as hers. Having their cocks either in my mouth or up my backside and then being able to do the same to them too.

With my being a cuckold, I accepted this for it gave me a new meaning to sex by now being bi-sexual and having the pleasure of sucking on an erect male organ as well having mine sucked and getting fucked in such a pleasurable way that made life worth living.

THE END

Here is a sample from another story you may enjoy:

Me, Carol and Raoul

Bi Romance Erotica

Amy Redek

CAROL IS my adopted daughter. She was just four years old when her parents died in a car crash while we were living in Saudi Arabia. We, being Carol herself, her parents and myself and my wife Maureen.

My name is Daniel Turpin, though ever since I first went to school, I was given the nickname of Dick because of my surname being that of a famous highway robber. It was in college that I met my wife whilst studying to be an engineer, specifically that that involved oil plants, the constructions and so forth. Maureen was there studying Arabic which fitted in nicely with both of us wanting to work in Arabia where the money was good.

For two years whilst in college, we were inseparable with me really courting Maureen and eventually proposed marriage to her which she accepted and we would get married after receiving our diplomas from the college. This came to pass and we then were married in her local church before we moved to London where I had been offered a job with a large petroleum company and so Maureen obtained a position in the London University, teaching Arabic.

We were there in London for two years, and during that time, we tried to produce a child between us, but failed. Then taking the bull by the horns, I went and had my sperm checked and though I was relieved to find that I was fertile, meant that it was Maureen who had the problem. I didn't tell her then that I was okay and waited for her to be checked out, not wanting her to refuse to be checked.

She broke down in tears when she read the letter of her results, and it took me some time to console her, telling her that I still love her and we could always adopt a child and raise it as one of our family. She finally agreed to this suggestion though it was put on the back burner for a while as I was told by my firm that they wanted me to go out to Saudi Arabia to oversee a petroleum plant that they wanted constructed out there.

It was an offer that I couldn't refuse, what with the salary being nearly three times what I was getting then. The plus side was that Maureen was also offered a place in a local school where I would be working from, to teach the children English because of her expertise in their language.

So off we went and I spent eight months in the planning of the refinery while Maureen really only worked part time at the school. To fill in the gap between school classes, she volunteered to help in the English enclave in the crèche.

This was where Carol had been put whenever her mother and father had to leave on business, where she would be looked after while they were away. If they were to be away for more than a day, Maureen was only too glad to take her into our dwelling till they returned. She was only three years old at the time and quite often stayed with us over the whole year.

It was a sad day to tell her that her parents would no longer be coming home and were surprised at how well she took this news of their death. I couldn't be spared the duty of seeing that the child went back to England, where her parents were to be buried, so Maureen took her.

It was on the flight that Maureen asked her if she would like to be adopted and live with us, which with some aplomb, Carol said she would like that. So after the funeral, Maureen saw the authorities and with not having any other relatives, saw that this could be agreed.

So while in London, all the necessary paperwork was done and so she became our adopted daughter. The fact that she had come to love staying with us when her parents were away, helped enormously, so that was how we came to have a daughter of our own.

The pair of them eventually returned to Saudi Arabia, me already having had quite a few phone calls with Maureen, having agreed to the adoption as I liked Carol too. I met them at the airport and even got a kiss from Carol after one from Maureen.

'Can I call you daddy now?' were Carol's first words to me there.

'By all means Carol. I am now your daddy and will help your mummy to see that you enjoy yourself.' For this, I got another kiss on the cheek.

So we stayed in Saudi for the eight years it took the construction firm to finish building the plant and when done, I was asked to stay on for at least a couple of years more to see that everything ran smoothly. Though I did return to England twice in that period. The first was for my father's funeral, and the second, for my mother's.

Maureen had stayed behind because of Carol, though it wasn't long before I was left with Carol for Maureen to do the same journey to see her father being buried. She had consoled me when my parents had died and now it was my turn to console her. Little did we know that she would be returning within the year for her mother's funeral.

Carol and I took her to the airport and kiss our goodbyes before we waved her off, not knowing that we would never see her again. It was two days later that I was told that her plane had crashed into the sea and there were no survivors.

Our house was like a morgue for the following few days, both of us crying and consoling each other that I had lost my wife and she had lost her mother. Only there wasn't a visit to England this time as the bodies from the crash were not recovered, Carol was now sixteen and had finished her schooling and so became the mistress of the house, seeing to the food and washing etc., while I despondently carried on working.

Though only for six months, having had enough of the place and requested to be released to return to England to get all my affairs in order. It was with reluctance that it was agreed and so Carol and I left Saudi Arabia for the last time.

My parents had left me their old home just outside of London and it surprised me at how much money had been left to me too. There was also another surprise waiting for me in the form of a phone call from a bank in London for me to call upon about the will that had been left with them in respect of Maureen. I duly went there and the long shot of it was that I now had been left all that Maureen had been left to her by her parents.

What with having two valuable properties plus the money from both sides meant that I didn't need to work for the rest of my life. So both the houses left to me were sold and I had Carol with me when we then bought a house in London for her to join the London University and me to sort myself out as to what I should now do with myself having resigned from working the petroleum firm, now heating oil.

Carol was now seventeen years old with me being thirty eight, and at a loss as to what to do with myself in the coming years. It was only Carol that kept my feet firmly on the ground for the whole of the next year and the only thing to look forward to was her eighteenth birthday.

This duly came round and I was at a loss as what to buy her for this momentous period of her life. I mulled it over for a few days and could only come up with one idea. This I made known to her on the day in question.

The day arrived and I went downstairs where she was preparing breakfast, already knowing that she would be going to the University on this day.

'Good morning and a very happy birthday, Carol,' I said as we met in the dining room, and I gave her a kiss on the cheek.

'Thank you, daddy,' was the reply with a big smile.

'Now here's your birthday card and a small present for the moment as I have had another idea for another one,' I told her as I passed over the card and a small box.

'Thank you, daddy,' she said and read what I had written in the card. 'How lovely,' and came over and gave me another kiss, though this surprised me for the kiss was on my lips...

If you enjoyed this sample then look for **Me, Carol and Raoul**

Also by this Author

The Painted Sword

Cruise Control

Wild Pleasures

Lending My Beloved

Lady of Cuckolds

Lady of Pleasure

Lady Magenta

Sexually Overdosed

Meeting My Fancy Dear

Prison Sex Slave

Chasing A Shadow

The Hostel

The Island

Thirst for Drugs and Pleasure

Forgotten Identity

Grey Memories

Chronos: Time Machine

The Hard Bomber

Honeymoon Abduction

The Yacht Sins

Summer at the Villa

Practice Makes Perfect

Stranger Danger

Following Father's Footsteps

The Square Circle

The Wizard of Kos

Out in the Real World

Me, Carol and Raoul

Also by this Author

The Painted Sword

Cruise Control

Wild Pleasures

Lending My Beloved

Lady of Cuckolds

Lady of Pleasure

Lady Magenta

Sexually Overdosed

Meeting My Fancy Dear

Prison Sex Slave

Chasing A Shadow

The Hostel

The Island

Thirst for Drugs and Pleasure

Forgotten Identity

Grey Memories

Chronos: Time Machine

The Hard Bomber

Honeymoon Abduction

The Yacht Sins

Summer at the Villa

Practice Makes Perfect

Stranger Danger

Following Father's Footsteps

The Square Circle

The Wizard of Kos

Out in the Real World

Me, Carol and Raoul

About the Author

George Eliot was a famous writer, though at the time, only male authors were recognised. It was in fact the pen name of Mary Ann Evans, a female.

When I started writing, I thought that if a woman could use a male name, why, with me being male, why couldn't I use the name of a female? Though to be different, I made my writer's name from an anagram of my real name.

I wasn't the brightest spark in my school days and it was only while being in the Merchant Navy did I self-educate myself. That being mostly literature, classical music and artists, like Tolstoy, Chopin and Rembrandt. After leaving the navy, I had several jobs, finishing up by being a working boss using my own maxim that 'Management is the art of delegation.'

It's when I became self-employed that I began to write, though sadly, not many of my books can be published because of certain laws that forbid certain aspects of life. This never fazed me for I was really writing just to please myself having a wide range of the human psych.

Having written ninety stories, my only aim now is to reach one hundred. I give thanks to the publishers for at least putting some of my efforts out for others to enjoy as much as I did in the writing of them.

From the Author

Check my page on Amazon and my blog for Updates and interesting info.

Author Central – http://www.amazon.com/Amy-Redek/e/B00A48NQ72
Author Blog – http://amy-redek.awesomeauthors.org/

If you enjoyed any of my books then please share the love and click like on my books in Amazon.

If you write me a review and send me an email I will send you a free book, or many.
(Just know that these emails are filtered by my publisher.)

Good news is always welcome.

One Last Thing, For Kindle Readers...

When you turn the page, Kindle will give you the opportunity to rate this book and share your thoughts on Facebook and Twitter. If you enjoyed my writings, would you please take a few seconds to let your friends know about it? Because... when they enjoy they will be grateful to you and so will I.

Thank You!

Amy Redek
amy_redek@awesomeauthors.org